Montana
★ MAVERICKS™

**Stories of family and romance
beneath the Big Sky!**

"I need something from you, Cleo."

"Me?" Her voice sounded breathless. "What could I possibly do for you?"

"You could marry me."

Marry him. Marry Ethan.

Cleo's heart lurched, as if it was trying to find a way out of her chest. "Are you kidding?" she said.

"Not kidding."

Marry Ethan? This whole episode was like something out of a fantasy, a too-familiar fantasy born the first moment she saw Ethan last winter. But the reality of Ethan was right in front of her. She could smell his delicious, sophisticated scent and see new lines of tiredness, or grief, maybe, etched around his serious mouth. His sister had died. He had a baby now.

A husband. A child. Ethan. A fantasy come to life.

"Yes, Ethan. I'll marry you."

CHRISTIE RIDGWAY

The Marriage Maker

Published by Silhouette Books

America's Publisher of Contemporary Romance

Special thanks and acknowledgment to Christie Ridgway
for her contribution to the Montana Mavericks series.

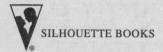 SILHOUETTE BOOKS

ISBN-13: 978-0-373-36233-2

THE MARRIAGE MAKER

Copyright © 2000 by Harlequin Books S.A.

Recycling programs
for this product may
not exist in your area.

Visit Silhouette Books at www.eHarlequin.com

Printed in U.S.A.

CHRISTIE RIDGWAY

Native Californian Christie Ridgway started reading and writing romances in middle school. It wasn't until she was the wife of her college sweetheart and the mother of two small sons that she submitted her work for publication. Many contemporary romances later, she is the happiest when telling her stories despite the splash of kids in the pool, the mass of cups and plates in the kitchen, and the many commitments she makes in the world beyond her desk.

Besides loving the men in her life and her dream-come-true job, she continues her longtime love affair with reading and is never without a stack of books. You can find out more about Christie or contact her at her website, www.christieridgway.com.

To my editor, Lynda Curnyn.
Thanks for everything.

Prologue

Never in her life had Cleo Kincaid Monroe schemed to get a kiss.

"But there's a first time for everything," she muttered to herself as she moved around the spacious kitchen of the Big Sky Bed & Breakfast.

"Did you say something?" The deep voice of Ethan Redford, her evening's date, came from the direction of the small den off the kitchen.

"Say something? Not me. Uh-uh. Nothing." And nothing was exactly what had happened between Cleo and Ethan. Not tonight when he'd taken her to dinner at the Whitehorn Country Club, not last week when he'd flown her in a private plane for lunch in Bozeman, not all the times they'd run into each other at the B and B where he was staying and where she lived with her mother and sister.

Cleo scooped coffee into an unbleached filter, vowing to change that nothing to something, to a kiss, because for the three weeks since Ethan had arrived in Whitehorn, Montana, she hadn't been able to think of anything *but* kissing him.

Aware that it was after midnight, she dumped another generous scoop of grounds into the filter and clicked on the coffeemaker. Drowsiness wasn't going to get in the way of this kiss, either, by gosh.

Another woman might have thought Ethan didn't *want* to kiss her, but Cleo figured it had more to do with all the interruptions that came with living at the family business. Why, after their Bozeman lunch they'd stood in this very kitchen and she'd actually *seen* the kiss in his eyes, even felt his warm breath rush across her mouth as he leaned toward her. But then her sister Jasmine and their mother had bustled in, wanting every detail of Cleo's first-ever private plane ride.

She could have killed them.

But tonight, ah, tonight the B and B was blissfully quiet. Ethan was their only guest right now—early February not being the high tourist season in Montana—and Jasmine went to bed early. Cleo cast a glance down the hall that led to the family's bedrooms and didn't see a light under her mother's door, either. That was good, too. Celeste hadn't been sleeping well lately and maybe she was finally getting a chance to catch up on her rest.

Cleo loaded a tray with the coffee carafe, mugs, cream, sugar and spoons, then took one bracing breath before stepping into the den.

And there he was.

Her stomach gave that funny little hiccup it always did when she looked at Ethan. There wasn't much call for elegant dark business suits, white shirts and ties in Montana, but Ethan wore them with the ease most of the men she knew wore down jackets and cowboy boots.

He'd thrown his suit jacket over the rocking chair in the corner, rolled up his sleeves and loosened his tie. Cleo's tummy hiccuped again. Who'd have thought "corporate rumple" could look so delicious and complement so well that glint of gold stubble on his chin?

She let her gaze wander up to his blue eyes. Guilt pinged her. "You look tired," she said, and here she was, ready to feed him megadoses of caffeine to satisfy her own sensual curiosity. She knew he'd been working long hours on a merger deal between the local ATI Com company and the Kyoto-based Sokia Industries.

But he smiled—grinned really, that confident Ethan grin—and stood to take the tray out of her hands. "It wears a man out, talking about himself all night." He set the tray on the small table in front of the love seat he'd been sitting on. "Don't think I didn't realize you were plying me with questions."

With her hands unoccupied, Cleo found herself suddenly nervous. The den was small and the love seat—the only sitting space available since Ethan's jacket occupied the rocking chair—was even smaller. She swallowed as he sat back down, his tall frame taking up more than half of the cushions. "My questions were legitimate," she said, trying to hide her nervousness with a smile. "I didn't know a thing about a merger and acquisitions consulting company."

He grimaced. "And now you probably know more than you ever wanted to…and about the man who owns one."

Cleo remained standing, her hands clutching each other. Yes, Ethan had told her about his company, United Mergers, Inc., and about the deal he was trying to put together here in Whitehorn. He'd told her about his penthouse condo in Houston and about the constant travel his work required. But did she know much about *him?* He hadn't shared one word with her about his personal life. A little shiver of apprehension tickled her spine. Maybe kissing Ethan wasn't such a good idea, after all.

"Are you cold?" Ethan patted the love seat beside him. "Come and sit down and let me warm you up with some…coffee."

Was Cleo imagining that little hesitation? What about that little gleam in his eye? "Maybe…" She glanced back toward the kitchen, as if some excuse might conveniently present itself.

"Cleo." Two of his fingers curled in her direction, more commanding than coaxing. "Come here."

That shiver sped down her spine again, but there was no saying no to the decisive tone in Ethan's voice. She didn't want to, anyway, of course. Not really. Not when she'd been staring into his intense blue eyes all evening. Not when she'd been wondering for days what his crisp, dark gold hair would feel like between her fingers.

She slid onto the cushion beside him, pressing against the upholstered arm. To hide her nervousness, she busied herself arranging the soft gathers of her long, violet-colored, thermal-knit dress. Small buttons ran from the hem to the modest neckline, and Ethan reached out and touched the topmost one, right below the pulse beat at her throat.

"This dress matches your eyes," he said quietly. "Did I tell you tonight how beautiful you look?"

Goose bumps prickled her skin and she felt her cheeks heat. She kept her gaze on her lap. "I think you mentioned it, right after you noticed the green fingerpaint in my hair."

He leaned forward and picked up a long wavy tendril of the stuff in question. The green had been quite a startling contrast to its usual russet color. Cleo couldn't believe she'd missed it when she'd gotten ready for their date. But even then, the idea of kissing Ethan had been distracting her.

He idly toyed with her hair, brushing the end against her cheek with a teasing flick. "Occupational hazard, right?"

"I suppose so." As the director of Beansprouts, Whitehorn's only day care center, fingerpaint was merely one of life's daily surprises. She grinned. "But I tell you, a couple of occupational-type presents made up for it. Brandon Rye brought me some fat earthworms from his family's compost bin along with a big ol' sloppy kiss."

Ethan's hand, still tickling her with her hair, froze midstroke. "A sloppy kiss? And who is this Brandon? Should I be jealous?"

Cleo looked up at Ethan then. Her cheeks burned and her heart pounded, but she didn't let either sensation stop her. "I don't know if you should be jealous," she answered. "Are you?"

He smiled, and grooves appeared in his lean cheeks. "That depends on whether you like sloppy kisses."

Cleo liked to breathe, but it didn't appear she'd get air soon, not with how it all seemed to be sucked away by the contrast of Ethan's playful smile with his intense, darkening gaze. "I…like all kinds of kisses."

Ethan's smile died and the heat in his eyes intensified. "Is that right?" He leaned closer.

Cleo watched his face near hers, her heart pounding hard and loud. The kiss. It was coming. And the idea scared her all over again so she put her hand lightly on his chest to slow his obvious intent. "Ethan…" she said.

His gaze was trained on her lips. "Hmm?"

It was the first thought that popped into her head. "Brandon's three years old."

That cocky, confident Ethan grin flashed again. "Cleo?"

"Hmm?"

He cupped her face with both his big hands. "I'm not."

Then he touched her mouth.

His lips were warm and his scent spicy and she breathed him in, her stomach hiccuping again in excitement.

He held her face firmly with his hands, his fingertips against the pulses pounding at her temples. He angled his mouth to taste her deeper, but it was a gentle, thorough taking, his lips persuasive as his tongue slid softly into her mouth.

It was Ethan making a deal, she thought fuzzily as he curled his tongue coaxingly against hers. Smooth and slow, but ruthless, too. He trailed one hand from her face down her throat and held her there, too, the pulse at her throat beating against the vee made by his thumb and index finger. Goose bumps followed his path and Cleo found herself crowding his mouth, trying to press harder.

But he refused to be hurried, instead backing off a little himself and continuing to stroke his tongue softly, slowly—too soft, too slow—into her mouth.

She made a little sound of frustration and then finally remembered she had her own ways of getting what she wanted. Her fingers flattened against his shirtfront and she let him have that slow kiss as she explored the crispness of his shirt until she slid two fingers between the buttons beneath his tie.

She stroked once. Hot skin. She stroked twice. Hot male skin.

Ethan groaned, and then he widened her mouth with his and slid his tongue fully, wildly, inside.

Another rush of heat ran through Cleo, speeding from where their mouths met to run between her aching breasts. She took her free hand and touched the back of his head, pulling him closer with her palm against his thick golden hair.

He grunted and she made him pay for those three weeks of thinking of kissing by taking what she wanted—a slow pass of her tongue against his. She felt him shudder, and then she did, too, because he took her breasts in the curved cups of his palms.

Someone broke the kiss, and they stared at each other. Ethan's nostrils flared and there was a flush on his cheekbones. Cleo couldn't catch her breath;

it just heaved in and out, pushing her breasts against the palms of Ethan's hands.

With slow intent, he dropped his gaze, and she watched him watch himself rub his thumbs across her beaded nipples.

Cleo jerked, startled by the sweet sensation, surprised by how, how much she craved Ethan's touch.

He looked back up and met her eyes. "I'm going to see you," he said, his voice full of the kind of conviction that probably made CEOs in business meetings roll over and play dead.

Cleo didn't even have that much will. She only knew she wanted what Ethan wanted, his gaze on her, his hands on her. *Please.*

Never hurrying, not appearing the least bit nervous, his fingers started on the row of small buttons holding her dress together.

Cleo closed her eyes. There were too many buttons. He was taking too long. And then he peeled the dress off her shoulders.

Ethan groaned one more time. "Cleo. Hell. Cleo."

Her eyelids lifted and she saw his body was tense. He was looking at her breasts, and so she looked, too. Between the parted violet fabric of her clingy dress showed the lace of her darker violet bra, and rising from that was the swell of her breasts, taut and trembling.

Ethan's hands tightened on her shoulders. He

leaned forward, kissed her mouth hard, ran his tongue along her bottom lip.

Cleo shivered, only aware of how badly she wanted him to touch her. "I usually don't…" she said, feeling almost bewildered by the power of the wanting. "I'm not—"

Ethan kissed her swiftly again, then rested his forehead against hers. "I know. And I wish—"

The distant sound of glass breaking cut him off.

Cleo jerked and half rose from her seat. Another sound—a woman's stifled cry—made her rise completely. "My mother."

Ethan hastily stood, too, and he pulled Cleo's dress together, trying to button it. He looked around wildly, as if searching for an intruder or some other explanation. "What could it be?"

She pushed his hands away and quickly fastened the most crucial buttons as she ran through the kitchen. "A nightmare," she called back, now speeding down the hall. "She has terrible nightmares."

Cleo threw open the door to her mother's bedroom. Just as she expected, Celeste was awake. With the help of the dim hallway light, Cleo confirmed her mother had had another run-in with the terrible dream. Tears still ran down Celeste's pretty face.

"Don't come in!" she ordered.

Cleo grabbed the doorjamb to halt her forward momentum. "What? Why?"

Instead of answering, Celeste struck a match, her

hand wavering with nightmare aftershocks as she lit the candle that was always at the ready on her bedside table.

The scent of Louisiana—that was how Celeste always described the aroma of her special white candles—filled the air. In the light the flame gave off, the light that Celeste believed burned the dream's evil from the room, Cleo saw why her mother had ordered her to stay by the door.

Somehow she'd broken the delicate glass vial that always sat on the small bedside table, as well. In the incongruous shape of a skeleton, the vial had been filled with bergamot oil. Inspired by her time on the bayou, Celeste conferred upon the oil a special power, just as she did the candles. She believed rubbing the stuff on her skin would ease the almost-arthritic cramping of her left hand that invariably followed the horrible dream.

Cleo watched her mother take a long, deep breath. "Are you all right, Mama?"

Celeste closed her eyes, opened them, and a faint smile moved the corners of her mouth. "I'm all right for now, Cleo."

"I'll get a broom." Her heart heavy, she whirled around, and headed back toward the kitchen.

To find Ethan lingering by the sink with his back to her, staring out into the snowy February night.

Cleo automatically lifted her fingers toward the remaining undone buttons of her dress.

Ethan turned around, catching her.

She froze.

His gaze flicked in the direction of her breasts, flicked back to her face. He swallowed. "Is everything all right?"

Cleo self-consciously dropped her hands to her sides. "She has a recurring nightmare that is very… unsettling."

"Ah." He shoved his hands into the pockets of his slacks. "Please tell her I'm sorry."

"I will." Cleo backed toward the utility closet where they stored the broom. "And, um, Ethan." Her cheeks burned. She wondered if he would want to wait for her to settle her mother back to sleep. She wondered if she had the nerve to ask him to wait. "I'm, uh, sorry, too."

His mouth curved up but there was no smile in his eyes or his voice. "Don't worry about it." He took a step in the direction that would take him to the guest stairs and his second-floor bedroom. "Good night, Cleo."

Good night, Cleo. Her courage didn't show itself to ask him for something more than that. Biting her bottom lip, she just watched him head out of the kitchen.

"Wait!" Her voice was squeakily anxious.

Ethan halted, then slowly turned around. One dark gold eyebrow rose. "What?"

Cleo swallowed. "Before…before…" She gave up

and just gestured toward the den and the love seat that she'd never look at quite the same way again. "Back there, back then, you…" Impatient with herself, she ran a hand through her hair. "You were saying something. What was it?"

Ethan's expression didn't give any of his thoughts away. Cleo supposed his kind of work made that an important trait, too. "Tomorrow, Cleo. We'll talk tomorrow."

And this time when he turned toward the stairs, Cleo let Ethan go. *Tomorrow.*

But when tomorrow came, Ethan Redford left the Big Sky B and B, without a word of cxcuse or explanation to anyone. As a matter of fact he disappeared from Montana altogether, leaving Cleo with only two imprints as a reminder of him—one of his credit card and the other of his kiss.

One

The thirty-year-old nightmare was older than Celeste Kincaid Monroe's daughter Cleo, but it gripped Celeste ruthlessly all the same, dragging her instantly from sleep to terror.

The bayou again. Moss hanging like sticky, gray spiderwebs in the trees. The scent of wet decay.

Thunder. Once. Twice.

Then, as always, he appeared, a dark figure carrying something even darker. Fear surged like adrenaline through Celeste's veins. It sang in her blood, an eerie, high-pitched dirge. She dug her bare toes into the mud.

Turn! Run!

But escape was impossible. The tall silhouette of her brother, Jeremiah Kincaid, kept coming toward her, the water swishing around his knees. The burden in his arms didn't seem to trouble him. He carried it to Celeste as if it were a gift.

"No, Jeremiah," she whispered. No, he shouldn't be here in Louisiana. He'd never come to see her once she'd done his bidding and married Ty Monroe.

"Look," he said, his voice commanding her, always telling her how it was, what she must do. "Look what is yours."

"No." She kept her gaze away from the limp body in his arms. It would be her sister Blanche, who had died after childbirth. It could only be Blanche, and Celeste refused to look at her. She couldn't bear to see her sister's vibrant fall of hair trailing through the stagnant, murky water. Just the thought made her heart stop, then disappear altogether.

In the cavern of her chest, only pain remained, echoing over and over.

"Look," Jeremiah insisted.

Fear again, with its high-pitched song. *No.* But then she obeyed, her gaze angling down, down, toward the dead body of—

No! Celeste jerked up her head…

…and jerked right out of the nightmare's grasp.

Lying against the soft sheets in her bedroom at Whitehorn's Big Sky Bed & Breakfast, Celeste tried to catch her breath as tears rolled down her cheeks. She wiped at them with her hands, then turned her face against the pillow. Still, the dream clutched at her.

"Montana," she whispered to herself, sitting up and lighting the white candle beside her bed. She'd left Louisiana with her husband after only a year, coming back to Whitehorn and buying this house on the lake that with her sister Yvette she'd turned into the Big Sky Bed & Breakfast. This was where her daughters were born and lived. Montana.

Forget the dream. But despite the steady, bright flame of her candle, the emotions the dream always roiled up still lurked in the dark corners of the room. She shivered.

And the past. The past lurked, too, hovering above her bed like a dark cloying canopy.

Celeste threw off the covers. Though her clock said it was only 5:00 a.m., she wasn't going to find any more sleep. Dressing in jeans, sweater and lambskin boots, Celeste told herself a cup of coffee would burn away any last traces of the bad dream.

She quickly made up the bed, blew out her candle, then stepped into the hall, shutting her bedroom door firmly. Just as decisively, she shoved the memory of the dream to the back of her mind.

She couldn't help being a victim to her nights, but she refused to let her waking hours be tainted, too. Today she wouldn't let the one emotion that always stayed with her after the nightmare—that one unnameable emotion—overshadow her every daytime hour.

Celeste took the long route to the kitchen,

walking through the public rooms of the B and B as if inspecting the intricate, natural-hued woodwork of the arts-and-crafts-style house could bring her quickly and fully into the present. Through the large living room windows she could see the last of the stars reflected in the glassy surface of Blue Mirror Lake. She stared out at the water, her hands absently stroking the Native-print blanket thrown over the back of one of the room's rattan couches.

After the years she'd spent alongside the bayou in Louisiana, this house, overlooking the water of the small natural lake, had drawn her, and not just because it was a respectable distance from the controlling influence of her brother, Jeremiah Kincaid. She'd always been grateful to her late husband Tyler's agreeing to return to Montana and to buy this property. He'd recognized that she'd needed something to call her own, especially when he travelled so often. And the house was a true gem. There were a few others scattered among the pines surrounding the lake—vacation places, all of them—and most newer than her three-story house. It had been an ideal location to raise a family, an ideal home for her and Yvette to turn into a ten-bedroom bed-and-breakfast, and an ideal way to support themselves while they also raised Summer, the orphaned daughter of their sister Blanche.

Blanche.

Celeste shivered as that dream-born emotion she

was trying to bury struggled to surface. She hurried away from it by hurrying out of the room, past two more rattan couches and overstuffed club chairs, through the massive dining room with its long mission-style table and heavily beamed ceiling.

Letting herself think only of coffee, she swore she could almost smell it as she pushed the swinging door that led into the kitchen.

Celeste blinked in the dazzling overhead light. The room was bright, there *was* coffee already brewed, and she wasn't going to keep her insomnia a secret because it seemed another Monroe woman shared it.

"Mama!" Celeste's twenty-seven-year-old daughter Cleo looked up from the mug she'd been frowning at.

"Sweetie, what's wrong?" Celeste crossed the hardwood floor in the direction of the scarred oval table where Cleo was sitting. "You're looking at that coffee as if it's your worst enemy."

Cleo's full lips raised in something that wasn't quite a smile. "It is *my* coffee, after all, Mama, not Jasmine's."

Well, her younger daughter was undoubtedly a master in the kitchen, but Celeste knew Cleo was just avoiding the real question. "C'mon, sweetie, this is your mother you're talking to. You don't usually have trouble sleeping."

Cleo's eyebrows came together in concern. "No,

it's you that usually can't get any rest. Another nightmare?"

Celeste gestured with her hand as if to brush the subject away. She didn't want to discuss it. "I'm asking what's keeping you awake."

There was a long pause, then Cleo looked balefully back down at her coffee mug. "Beansprouts. I'm worried about the day care center."

Celeste let the admission go for a moment and moved to the counter to pour herself some of Cleo's less-than-stellar coffee. She was proud of her daughter's success as the director of the day care center and knew that Cleo also took a lot of pride in what she did. The man she leased the building from had told Cleo last week he was going to sell the property as soon as possible. With her lease agreement up for renewal, Cleo had a legitimate worry that her business might not survive.

"You haven't found another possible site, honey?" Celeste added a dash of milk to her mug then held the hot ceramic against the knuckles of her left hand. Their deep arthritic ache was as unpleasantly familiar as the dream that brought it about.

"Nothing," Cleo said, shrugging. "And Gene came by again yesterday. He's putting up a For Sale sign next week."

Celeste came forward to lay a hand on top of her daughter's head. "Maybe he won't find anyone interested in buying."

"Mmm."

Celeste's eyes narrowed. If she had to guess, she would say that Cleo wasn't thinking about Beansprouts or For Sale signs or anything to do with business. There was a sad, faraway but dreamy look in her daughter's beautiful violet eyes. "This is about something else. Something besides Beansprouts."

Cleo didn't look up.

Celeste's heart squeezed, and she used her aching left hand to tilt up her daughter's chin. "Oh, Cleo," she said. "This isn't about him, is it? He's been gone three months, sweetie. You wouldn't still be mooning over a man like Ethan Redford?"

A new voice broke in. "Of course Cleo's not mooning over Ethan, Mama. Cleo is much too sensible, much too practical to be letting a big shot, here-today-gone-tomorrow man like Ethan Redford even give her heart a tickle."

Celeste chuckled as her younger daughter Jasmine glided into the room. At twenty-three, with her short-cropped black hair and a slender face, she looked too fresh and wide-awake for five-thirty in the morning. "You're up early."

"Mmm." She took one sniff at the coffee carafe, grimaced in mock disgust, then dumped its contents into the sink. "Cleo would be in a better mood if she could learn to make better coffee."

Since Jasmine's coffee was universally acclaimed as fabulous—as well as anything else she created in the kitchen—neither Cleo nor Celeste bothered disagreeing with her. As a matter of fact, Cleo only said, "Sit down, Mama," and then took both their mugs to the sink. She poured out the contents, then set the cups on the counter to wait for her sister's heaven-blessed brew.

She gave Jasmine a significant look. "Mama had another nightmare."

Both young women turned toward her. Celeste froze under her daughters' worried gazes. "No—" But she stopped, because they were pointedly looking at her hands, and she realized she'd been massaging the painful left one with her right. She sighed.

"Please, girls, let's talk about something else," she pleaded. Talking about her nightmare might allow that disturbing, unnameable emotion she was keeping under strict control to rise again. "Please."

Jasmine surrendered first, sliding her gaze toward her more voluptuous sister. "Okay, Mama." She grinned, that devilish grin of a younger sibling who knows just how to push the older one's buttons—and revels in it. "Let's talk about what's bugging Cleo."

"Watch it," Cleo threatened. "I can still hide your Barbie dolls, brat." She propped her hands on her hips.

Jasmine's grin widened. "I've hidden them from *you*. At your insistence, I recycle, Cleo. I compost our kitchen scraps. I'd never wear fur. But you're not going to make me give up my precious fashion dolls. Uh-uh."

Before Cleo could retort, the kitchen's back door opened and Frannie, Celeste's niece, stepped over the threshold. In a brown, knee-length business suit that matched the brown of her hair and the brown of her eyes, she looked completely prepared for another day in her job as a loan officer at the Whitehorn Savings and Loan.

At five-nine, Frannie towered over her cousins. In a familiar morning ritual, she automatically took the cup of coffee Cleo poured for her. "What are we talking about?" She lived at her parents' house, located just behind the B and B.

Jasmine started bustling around the kitchen, getting ready for the breakfast she'd serve the guests. "Fashion, I'd guess you'd say."

Frannie touched the brown tortoiseshell clip that held her hair at the back of her neck. She sighed. "I guess that lets me out, then."

Jasmine shook her head. "Only because you won't let me make you over, Frannie. If you'd just give yourself a chance, you'd be stunning."

Frannie flushed. "Let's talk about something else."

That mischievous smile twitched at Jasmine's lips again. Uh-oh, Celeste thought. Prepare yourself, Cleo.

"We could go back to discussing Cleo's love life," Jasmine said, taking eggs out of the refrigerator.

"Oh, no, you don't." Cleo's face blushed just as pink as Frannie's.

Jasmine acted as if she hadn't heard her. "Mama wondered if maybe Cleo was still smitten with that Ethan Redford who was here three months ago."

Frannie blinked owlishly. "Who?"

"You remember." Jasmine took the juicer out of a lower cupboard. "He took Cleo out a couple of times, and I admit the looks he gave her could have melted that old wallpaper off the downstairs hallway, but then he just—poof!—left Whitehorn. What do you think? Is Cleo in need of romantic repair?"

"Of course not." Frannie blinked again and her voice was absolutely certain. "Cleo is much, much too practical to make any kind of romantic mistake."

"Sensible, too. You missed sensible, Frannie," Cleo added. Her face had regained its normal color and her voice was without animation.

Something in the nonemotion of Cleo's voice niggled at Celeste and her mother radar went on the alert. "Cleo, sweetie—"

"Good morning!" The back door had opened again to admit Frannie's parents, Celeste's sister Yvette and her husband, Edward Hannon. The smell of a cool spring morning accompanied them as they headed for the countertop and Jasmine's coffee.

The girls exchanged pleasantries with the new arrivals, and soon they were all savoring their morning ritual. Jasmine continued preparing breakfast for the guests, but the rest of them took their places around the large kitchen table. Edward unfolded the newspaper and smiled at the faces circling him. "And a good morning it is. No better way for a man to start the day than with a glimpse of the harem that has kept him happy all these years."

Celeste joined the others in the groan that invariably accompanied Edward's usual comment. Someone wished that David, Frannie's brother, was around to keep his father in check.

Thinking of her nephew, Celeste could only wish David was nearby, too. An FBI agent in Atlanta, Georgia, he hadn't made it to Montana for a visit in too long. And she needed her loved ones around her. The nightmares were trying to tell her something about the past, and she felt certain she'd need all those she held dear when the day of reckoning came.

Yvette touched Celeste's arm. "Are you all right?"

"She had another rough night," Cleo said.

Celeste felt like a specimen in a bottle with five sets of serious eyes regarding her. That desperate, unnamed emotion swirled up inside her like a tornado, and she had to take a deep breath to find the strength to push it back down. "But I'm looking forward to an interesting day," she said firmly. "Edward, tell us some good news."

With one more searching look at her face, Edward smoothed the front page absently, then bent his head. "Well," he said, smoothing the paper again. "Lyle Brooks finally broke ground for that resort/casino complex he's been talking up all over town."

Celeste frowned. That young man was some sort of kin on the Kincaid side and she'd never felt comfortable around him. "But isn't the casino part of the Laughing Horse Reservation? How is Lyle involved?"

It was banker Frannie who answered. "Because Indian laws allow gambling, the casino will be on the Laughing Horse reservation, Aunt Celeste. But the accompanying resort will be on Kincaid land. Lyle's put together the financing for both projects." She didn't look any more at ease about the young man than Celeste felt. "In ten years the whole thing will move out of Kincaid/Laughing Horse hands and into those of a joint corporation, headed by Lyle."

Celeste should have been happy that they were off the subject of her nightmares, but suddenly the whole notion of Lyle and the disturbance of Kincaid land chilled her. A shiver racked her body. Yvette's hand moved across the table to cover Celeste's left one, the ache in it more pronounced than usual.

"Celeste, what's the matter?" Yvette asked.

Another shiver rattled over Celeste's spine. "There's just something about Lyle I don't like," she said to her sister. "Maybe it's because he reminds me of Jeremiah."

At the mention of their elder brother's name, silence fell around the table. When he'd been murdered, the violence had been shocking, but they hadn't mourned him. He'd been cold and controlling all his life.

Celeste took a long breath, sorry to have brought her brother's name into their warm circle. She looked from face to face, trying to gauge their moods. Edward and Yvette were concerned about her, she could see, while Frannie looked almost embarrassed. Standing behind Cleo, two worry lines bisected Jasmine's smooth forehead. And Cleo— her beautiful, motherly Cleo—looked ready to fight tigers on Celeste's behalf. But even underneath all her bristling protectiveness Celeste sensed in her older daughter another kind of sadness...

Yvette squeezed Celeste's hand. "We love you," she said.

Oh. And she loved them all and wanted them so much to be happy. With her right hand she lifted her coffee cup to her mouth, intent on moistening her throat to tell them so.

But the coffee sloshed over her hand instead, and she didn't even notice the slight scald, because suddenly that frightening maelstrom of emotion, that nightmare hangover, rose up within her once again. There was no controlling it.

She looked around at the faces of her family, but the feeling stayed, pulsing inside her.

It was powerful and dark and she finally, finally, knew its terrifying name.

The emotion that always remained with her after the horrible dream was…shame.

Celeste dropped her gaze, unable to meet the eyes of her caring, beloved family. Because just as certain as she was that it was shame trying to claw its way out of her heart, she was quite sure her family would condemn her if they knew that long ago she had…she had…

What?

Oh, God. Despite the acknowledgment of that feeling of shame, despite thirty years of terror-filled nights, Celeste just didn't know.

She didn't know what terrifying, shameful thing she had done.

Two

Ethan Redford sat in his newly purchased Range Rover outside Whitehorn, Montana's Beansprouts day care center. Out his tinted windows he had a perfect view of the center's fenced playground. Under the watchful gaze of several women he didn't recognize, little kids built sandcastles, slid down a wavy slide, made imaginary meals in a gaily painted playhouse. Pleasing though the sight was, Ethan's fingertips drummed the saddle-colored leather armrest.

He was stalling.

As humbling as the confession might be, he had to admit to himself that the idea of confronting Cleo Monroe after his abrupt, three-month absence was making his palms sweat. Hell! And this from a man who'd faced down his drunken, raging father at nine years old and brokered his first multimillion-dollar merger at thirty.

He rubbed his hands against his deliberately casual khaki slacks. Though the deal he wanted to propose today was the most important of his life, he knew it wasn't the moment for an Armani suit and his best silk tie. For Cleo, he needed to appear approachable instead of powerful. Friendly, not frightening.

Cleo.

As if thinking her name had summoned her, the woman he'd been fantasizing about for three months stepped from the back door of the stucco building onto the fenced play yard. Instantly she was surrounded, little kids clamoring for her attention, little hands patting her legs, little fingers grabbing her hands.

Kind of like what he wanted to do. Grabbing her sounded good to him, too.

Ethan closed his eyes and groaned, remembering the sweet, silky feel of Cleo's skin. He saw the voluptuous rise of her breasts over her lacy bra and felt again the tremors shaking her body as he brushed his thumbs over her nipples. He groaned again.

When he'd left Cleo that night, he'd considered himself pretty damn heroic for backing away from the wildfire of their mutual physical attraction. He hadn't wanted to lead her on. She was the marrying kind, and he wasn't. She deserved a man prepared for the type of family life she undoubtedly desired, and that hadn't been him, by any means.

Fate must be laughing its head off about right now.

To the faint echoes of its capricious guffaws, Ethan forced himself out of his car and then reached into the rear seat for what had brought him from Houston back to Whitehorn, back to Cleo. He wrestled a bit with the latch that released the baby carrier from its car seat base, letting loose a soft curse.

Guilt gave him a little jab and he quickly apologized to the blond, wide-eyed baby staring up at him. "Sorry, Jonah." And sorry to you too, Della. The boy's mother wouldn't appreciate the child's first word being something better suited to a locker room than a nursery. He took a breath, pushing away the pain that came when he thought of Della. The only thing he could do for her now was to take care of Jonah.

That was where Cleo came in.

At the reception desk inside Beansprouts, Ethan asked to speak with the center's director—Cleo. The young receptionist gave him a friendly smile and after rising from her chair to peek at Jonah, told Ethan they didn't take children until they were two years old. She would be happy to place his name on their waiting list.

Ethan bared his teeth in what he hoped would

pass for a smile, and mildly asked once again to see the Beansprouts director. When the still-friendly but outright curious receptionist gave in and showed him into a small office, she asked his name.

Ethan told her he wanted to keep it a surprise.

He sure as hell hoped Cleo liked surprises.

When she walked through the office door, it was obvious she didn't. As she caught sight of him, her feet stopped before the rest of her body did and she grabbed the doorjamb to keep herself from pitching forward. Expressions chased themselves across her face. Ethan couldn't separate them all—but the last one he read loud and clear.

It was as cool and distant as her voice. "Ethan Redford," she said as if he'd never tasted the hot wetness of her mouth. Then her gaze dropped to the infant carrier he held against his chest as if it were a shield. She blinked, shook her head a little, blinked again.

"Who? What?" Her cheeks flushed a deep pink. *"Oh,"* she said.

Oh? What did she mean by that significant *oh?* And then it hit him.

Uh-oh.

"The baby's not mine," he said quickly. But then he had to correct himself. "Well, he is mine, but—" From the look on her face this wasn't going well. He sighed. "It's complicated."

Cleo took a breath and Ethan pretended he wasn't

aware of the way her breasts pressed against the long-sleeved white T-shirt she wore. "What do you want, Ethan?"

He sighed again. "That's complicated, too." The smile he gave her was supposed to be charming, but she looked distinctly unmoved. "Could we talk?"

With a little roll of one of her shoulders, she fully entered the room and shut the office door behind her. Then she walked past him, the familiar, delicate flower scent of her perfume brushing by him nonchalantly. Cleo's T-shirt was tucked into a long denim skirt that showed off her small waist and rounded hips and he had to look away until she was completely seated behind her desk.

She linked her fingers on the surface of a blotter-size calendar full of notations in neat, rounded handwriting. "What would you like to say, Ethan?"

He'd like to say he wished like hell they'd not been interrupted by her mother's nightmare that evening. He'd like to say that he'd been thinking of her kisses, of her skin, of the beauty of her wavy, russet hair for the past three months. He'd like to say that even in the midst of grief and worry, the memory of her smile and laughter had been a warm beacon.

Instead he sat in a chair across from her, the infant carrier resting on his knees. "This is my nephew, Jonah," he said simply. "And the day I left your mother's bed-and-breakfast, I was called away because Jonah's mother, my sister, had been the victim of a carjacking."

One of Cleo's hands rose to cover her mouth.

He went on doggedly. It wasn't an easy story to tell. "I probably should have left you some word, or called you when I reached Houston, but all I could think about was Della and Jonah. She was in intensive care with head injuries and Jonah was missing."

"Oh, my Lord," Cleo whispered. Suddenly she wasn't in her chair, but kneeling beside Ethan, her attention focused on the baby. One fingertip stroked his nephew's downy head. Her gaze turned Ethan's way. In her violet eyes was the sudden awareness that his story didn't have a happy-ever-after. "But the baby was found."

Ethan nodded. "In an alley, in Della's abandoned car." His hand curled into a fist, as the useless waste of the tragedy cut through him again like an acid burn. "Two days later the carjacker was killed in a police shoot-out. A day after that, my sister died." His voice was hoarse.

"Oh, Ethan." Cleo's warm hand covered his fist and he closed his eyes, her touch soothing and so damn welcome. "You must have loved her very much."

"She was my little sister." He opened his eyes and saw Cleo still kneeling between Jonah and him, one hand touching his, one hand on the baby's hair, linking all three of them together.

Just as he knew she would.

"Tell me about her, Ethan. You never even mentioned to me you had a sister."

Guilt stabbed him again. When he'd been in Montana three months ago he'd been carefully impersonal with Cleo. To tell the truth, he was carefully impersonal with everyone, but Cleo was the kind of woman who invited you to bare your soul. And because he'd been interested only in baring her body, he'd steered completely clear of anything that would even vaguely hint of any deeper intimacy.

But things were different now. *Everything* was different. Not him, though. He hadn't changed. But his needs had. So that meant telling Cleo what she wanted to know.

He cleared his throat. "Della was twenty-nine years old. She worked for me, at my office in Houston."

Cleo looked at little Jonah and smiled. "Was she blond like you?"

He pictured his sister in his mind. Not as he'd last seen her, her head swathed in bandages, bruises on her face and tubes everywhere, but as she'd been before the carjacking. "She was tiny, shorter than you, and she did have blond hair. After Jonah was born, she cut it short as a boy's."

Cleo nodded solemnly. "Easy to take care of."

"*She* was easy to take care of." Ethan broke off, suddenly embarrassed. Yeah, he missed his sister, but he wasn't about to get all maudlin in front of Cleo.

Maybe she sensed his reluctance, because she turned her attention back to the baby. "How old is he?"

"Seven months," Ethan replied.

"And where's Jonah's father?"

"His *biological* father abandoned both Della and the baby before Jonah was born. They were engaged, but let's just say Della found it a little…distressing when Drake gave her a black eye instead of a welcome home kiss one evening." Ethan and Della knew a lot about black eyes and the kind of men who dispensed them.

"She decided that she and the baby were better off without him and he didn't put up a fuss." With Ethan there, backing Della up, the cowardly bastard wouldn't have dared.

"And now that Della's…gone?" Cleo asked quietly.

"As far as Drake's concerned, Della and Jonah were gone from his life a long time ago." Ethan paused, because now they were getting to the important part. "I'm Jonah's f—"

Damn. He ran his hand through his hair. It was hard to say the word because he'd never considered himself suited to the job.

Cleo rose and leaned against the back of her desk, smiling a little as she looked down at Ethan. "His f—?" she asked, her almost-teasing voice easing the moment. "His what? Feet? Fiddle? Filly?"

Ethan's lips twitched and his brows came together. "Correct me if I'm wrong, Montana lady, but this city boy seems to recall that a filly is a *female* horse, right?"

At her little nod he couldn't resist reaching out to stroke one finger against the back of her hand. "Well, now, Cleo, you gotta know I'm all man, don't you?"

Her face pinkened and she snatched her hand away, and for the first time in months, Ethan's mood lightened. Cleo. God, it was right to come back to her. When his lawyer had made what should have been an outrageous suggestion, he'd instantly thought of her, of her wavy hair, of her warm touch, of the way she looked at him.

And the lawyer's suggestion was what he had to tell Cleo about now. Jonah had drifted off to sleep and Ethan carefully moved the carrier to the carpet beside him. He casually rested his hands on the arms of his chair, though the situation he found himself in was anything *but* casual.

"I'm Jonah's family now," Ethan said. "Nothing and no one is going to take him away from me. Della named me as his legal guardian." He paused.

"I think I hear a but," Cleo said slowly.

He nodded. "After Della…died, I hired a nanny right away. I was able to postpone the deal I had going on here in Whitehorn, but there were a couple of others I couldn't put off. You know what that means."

"You were out of town a lot."

Ethan stared down at the sleeping baby. "Yes. But I was cutting my trips as close to the bone as possible and the nanny was working out fine. Then Drake's parents entered the picture."

"The baby's grandparents."

Ethan nodded. "They're rich, they're socially prominent and they don't think much of me as Jonah's…father since I'm away from him so much."

"But the nanny—"

"Isn't a mother." Ethan looked up into Cleo's unsuspecting but sympathetic violet eyes. "They're suing for custody of Jonah."

"Oh." Cleo kneeled again, putting one hand on Ethan's shoulder. They were face-to-face, and hers was full of concern and sadness. "I'm so sorry, Ethan."

He looked at her steadily, and suddenly she dropped her hand and jumped to her feet. "Well, well." Something was making her very nervous, and he wondered if she'd figured out what he was about to ask.

She swallowed. "So now you're back in

Montana," she said briskly. "The ATI Com-Sokia deal again?"

Ethan captured her hand and stood. "I've been thinking about another kind of merger altogether."

She swallowed again, but didn't say a word.

"I need something from you, Cleo."

"Me?" Her voice sounded breathless and her hand tried to slip from his. "What could *I* possibly do for you?"

Ethan held her fingers firmly. "You could marry me, Cleo."

Marry him. Marry Ethan.

Cleo's heart lurched, as if it were trying to find a way out of her chest. "Are you kidding?" she said, her voice sounding very far away.

Ethan's blue eyes were scarily solemn. "Not kidding."

Cleo's heart pitched again, like a boat ready to capsize. Marry Ethan? This whole episode was like something out of a fantasy, a too familiar fantasy born the first moment she'd seen Ethan last winter. A fantasy that had only grown in detail and proportion every time she'd encountered him after that.

But the reality of Ethan was right in front of her, too close, really. She could smell his delicious, sophisticated scent and see new lines of tiredness, or grief maybe, etched around his serious mouth. His sister had died. He had a baby now.

Little Jonah was real, too. Cleo looked down at the sweet baby, snoozing in his carrier. With his blond hair and the blue eyes she'd glimpsed, he could really *be* Ethan's.

A husband. A child. Ethan and Jonah.

"Cleo?" Ethan rubbed his thumb across the backs of her knuckles, and she suppressed a shiver. A fantasy couldn't come to life this easily. "What are you thinking?" he asked.

She swallowed. "Ethan, I need to know—"

A light knock on the office door interrupted her.

They both started and with the distraction Cleo was able to reclaim her hand. She moved away from Ethan and hoped she appeared calm.

"Come in," she called.

The door opened and Lynn, one of the caregivers on her staff, peeked in. "I'm sorry, Cleo, but Bessie had a fall and needs your expert touch in the bandage department." Lynn's gaze slid toward Ethan and her eyes widened. "That is, if you have the time."

"I always have time for Bessie," Cleo said, almost glad for the temporary reprieve. She smiled as Lynn escorted the four-year-old into the office.

Bessie had platinum-blond hair in pigtails and her eyelashes were spiked wet with recent tears. A painful-looking scrape slashed across one knee.

Cleo knelt by her side. "What happened, sweetie?" she said softly. Though Ethan had stepped out of the way, she continued to feel his gaze on her.

Bessie frowned fiercely. "Kenny G.," she said, her gravelly voice always a shocking contrast to her angelic features.

Lynn, who stood behind Bessie, must have seen the puzzlement on Ethan's face because she suddenly grinned his way and explained Bessie's statement. "Not the famous musician, mind you, but an infamous three-year-old. We have four Kennys at Beansprouts." Her fingers ticked them off. "Kenny E., Kenny K., Kenny T., and—" she paused, "—Kenny G."

Bessie's truckdriver voice took over. "Kenny G. pushed me down."

Lynn smiled in Ethan's direction again. "Kenny G. is currently having a time-out."

Cleo tamped down a little spurt of irritation at the other woman. There was no need for Lynn to explain things to Ethan, or to even be looking at him with such appreciation. But she focused on Bessie instead, brushing back a stray strand of the little girl's hair. "You're okay now, though?"

Bessie nodded and held out a bandage. "But I want you to put this on for me."

"Sure, hon." Cleo swung the little girl into her arms and sat her on the edge of her desk. With gentle hands she lifted Bessie's right leg and propped her sneakered foot against her own thigh. "Did Lynn clean this for you?"

Bessie looked as though she wanted to say "yes,"

but Lynn produced a bottle of hydrogen peroxide and a soft cloth. "She wanted you to do that, too."

"No problem, kiddo," Cleo said. "We'll get it taken care of pronto." She hadn't met a child yet who didn't detest getting his or her scrapes and cuts cleaned, but she also knew that handling it with confidence and without cringing was best for everyone.

Within moments she ensured the scrape was free of dirt and then she applied the bandage, the whole time chattering with Bessie about what was scheduled for the afternoon's snack and the new kitten in the little girl's household. Aware the entire time of Ethan's focus on her, Cleo was proud that her hands didn't shake once. She ended the first aid with her usual healing kiss on Bessie's forehead and then she took the little girl's light weight in her arms to lift her off the desk.

Bessie looked over Cleo's shoulder. "Who's that?" she asked in her improbably rough voice, pointing at Ethan.

"Um..." Cleo froze, and noticed that Lynn's expression was as curious as Bessie's. "That's Mr. Redford. He's my, uh, friend." She set the little girl on her feet.

"He's cute," Bessie said, and she gave a little wave then skipped out of the room.

Lynn backed out more slowly, her gaze flicking between Cleo and Ethan. "Well, I'll just, um..." She seemed to have forgotten who and what generated her paycheck. "I'll just…"

"Go watch the kids?" Cleo prompted.

Lynn sighed. "Yeah." But then, as if she couldn't help herself, she sent Cleo a thumbs-up sign before shutting the door behind her.

Cleo hoped her cheeks weren't as red as they felt when she turned to face Ethan. "I'm, uh, sorry about that."

An echo of that old, confident Ethan grin flashed over his face. "Why? One female says I'm cute and another appears to have given me her stamp of approval. I'm thinking that's good for my case."

Apparently his proposal wasn't just a daydream, after all. Cleo leaned against her desk, gripping the edges with tight fingers. Marriage to Ethan! But as appealing as the idea was…

She inhaled a long, deep breath. "Why me?"

His eyes widened. "Uh." He shoved his hands in his pockets as he retreated to the far side of the small room, where he leaned his shoulders against the wall. "'Why you'?" he echoed.

Cleo tightened her grip on the edge of her old oak desk. "It's a hard question?"

"No. Yes." He groaned and pushed his hands impatiently through his hair.

Cleo had never seen the golden locks so disordered, not even the night she'd touched them herself as they'd kissed. She ignored the little hot rush of her blood at the memory. "Talk to me, Ethan," she said quietly.

His fingers raked through his hair once again. "My attorney in Houston—the one handling Della's estate and all the legalities regarding Jonah—he's very experienced in custody issues."

Cleo nodded. Ethan was no fool and money was no object. He'd hire the best.

"The Covingtons—Jonah's grandparents—have a lot of influence in Houston. If it comes to a court battle, they have the time and the money. To ensure I keep Jonah the attorney thought I needed something better than fat bank accounts, a trust fund for Jonah, and a top-ranked nanny. He thought I needed—"

"A wife." Cleo wasn't a fool, either.

"A mother for Jonah," Ethan corrected quickly.

Cleo's blood was running cooler now, but there was still hope in her heart. "That still doesn't explain why you came to see me, Ethan. Certainly you know plenty of women in other places. Someone from Houston, for example."

He shifted uncomfortably. "Cleo…"

"I never thought you were a man who didn't appreciate your share of women, Ethan."

He shifted again. "Sure, I have 'appreciated' women, but it's not like I have a harem of them all dying to wear my ring."

Cleo wanted to disagree, certain there were several—if not dozens—of women who wouldn't say no to Ethan. Women who'd be thrilled to wear his ring.

Such as herself.

Without warning, she remembered again that night on the love seat in the little den. She remembered how needy she'd been for him, how her pulse leaped when he'd touched her with his big hands. How she'd craved to have all of him against all of her.

No man had ever made her so excited and so hungry. And now she could have it all if she agreed to wear his ring. But still…

"You're in Montana, Ethan. Looking for a wife in my office. Please, just say it. Why me?"

"Because you're perfect, Cleo."

Her heart went crazy again, hopping around like a high school cheerleader. She released her grip on the desk, just about to launch herself into his arms.

"Because you're so…capable."

Capable? Cleo's heart tripped, and then fell with a long *whoosh*. Going cold, hot, cold, she sagged back against the desk, but he didn't seem to notice.

Instead Ethan smiled at her and continued. "You see, you're a childcare provider. How ideal is that? You have the education and the experience to be an unbeatable mother. My attorney couldn't be happier."

"Your attorney is happy?"

Ethan smiled wider and nodded. "'Unbeatable mother material.' Those were his exact words."

"What about a wife?" she said quietly, her words tinged with just a bit of sharpness. "What kind of wife material do you suppose I am?"

Ethan looked suddenly wary and he tried to step back, but his heel hit the wall with a soft *thump*. "Cleo, I—"

"What kind of wife material do you suppose I am, Ethan?" she asked again, her voice steelier this time.

He looked down at his hands for a moment, as if the answer might be written on them. Then he looked back up, his blue eyes guarded. "You're a practical, capable, sensible woman, Cleo. I think you make fine wife material or I wouldn't be here."

Capable. Practical. Sensible.

Maybe it was because she hadn't slept well the night before—she hadn't slept well in three months—that the words sounded more like insults instead of flattery.

Ethan needed a mother for Jonah and she had the right credentials. Ethan was willing to take a wife to get that mother, and she fit the bill because she was practical, capable, sensible.

Was that really the best thing anyone could say about her? It certainly echoed the sentiments her mother, sister and cousin had expressed this morning. Everyone was so darn certain that Cleo was sensible and practical.

Or maybe she was really just boring.

She crossed her arms over her chest, suddenly mad at the world, but especially mad at Ethan, her family, herself. What kind of woman gave a man the impression she'd be swayed by "practical" and "capable" and "sensible"?

She took a fast breath through her nose. "No," she said.

He blinked. "No, what?"

Cleo stared at him. What an idiot. "No, I won't marry you."

He blinked again. "Cleo——"

"Go find someone else, Ethan." She cast a look at Jonah and found herself softening when she saw the baby's sweet round cheeks and silky eyebrows. So she looked back at the rotten, gorgeous, and unpleasantly surprised Ethan.

Practical. Sensible. Ugh. "Goodbye," she said briskly.

"Goodbye?" he echoed stupidly.

"Goodbye."

He swallowed. "We can't talk about this some more?" He came toward her and she backed around her desk. "If not now, sometime later?"

So what that he was so darn good-looking he made her heart flutter? "*No.* I'm too busy. I have Beansprouts to run. Children, the staff." She looked out the window and remembered the most pressing problem. "I have to find a new building. My lease is running out and this one is up for sale."

Without waiting for him to answer, she sat in her chair and pulled a list of phone numbers from her desk drawer. "If you'll excuse me, Ethan." She put her hand on the phone.

He could be as belligerent as she. "What if I won't?"

She refused to look at him, even for one last time. "Please," she said.

A long, tense pause and then there was a flurry of movement and firm footsteps. Her office door opened, closed.

The room was without Ethan.

Cleo instantly folded, bending over to rest her flushed cheek on the cool desktop. Hot tears stung her eyes and she was unsure whether she was elated or disappointed that Ethan had given up.

Three

It was past 6:00 p.m. and Cleo was still sitting at her desk. The last Beansprouts's child had been picked up and the last staffer had gone home. She told herself she was taking advantage of the unfamiliar quiet to catch up on her bottomless stack of paperwork, but the only paper she'd put pencil to was a leaf from one of her "list pads"—stacks of tear-off sheets preprinted with lines.

Cleo had more list pads than most women had shoes. Yellow ones edged with flowers, white ones with a teacher's apple bulleting each line item; list pads printed on graph paper with thick, no-nonsense lines of military blue.

A sheet of that pad lay in front of her now, and she would have sworn she was just doodling as she stared out her window at the May twilight, but then she looked down. Her "doodles" were words, and what she'd really created was a list of the many practical, sensible things she'd done with her life.

Line one listed "Accounting 303." That was the class she'd taken the summer between her junior and senior years at college. A group of her friends had invited her to join them traveling through Europe for three months, but she'd needed the accounting class to graduate and it was hard to get into during the regular school year. So she'd taken the wise, practical route and given up Paris for profit-and-loss statements and the Alps for accounts receivable and payable.

Part of that same group of friends had urged her to join them in an Internet startup business after they graduated. That was why she'd written "Refused Internet Startup" on the second line. It hadn't seemed a safe choice, not when it meant moving to Las Vegas, of all places, and not when it meant they'd all be dirt-poor at the beginning. In the end—two years later—of course, that group of friends spent half the year vacationing in Europe. They'd struck it rich.

Next she'd written "Lives At Home." Cleo sighed. As much as she loved her family, it did seem as though a twenty-seven-year-old might want to have her own place. But it was so practical to live at home. Sensible.

Lastly were the words "Yearly Lease." She sighed

again. When she'd opened Beansprouts two years ago she'd been relieved to sign up for a mere twelve-month lease. That way, if the business didn't fly, she wouldn't be chained to a monthly payment for too long. She'd done the same the following year, even though by then the day care center had a foot-long waiting list.

Irritated at herself, Cleo tapped her pencil against the desktop. The building's owner, Gene, would have let her sign for something longer, but she'd wanted to be practical. Sensible. Just look where that had led her—to Gene suddenly wanting to sell and Cleo suddenly facing disaster.

She jumped up from her chair, depressed by the turn of her thoughts. Thanks to that annoying man, Ethan Redford, she was viewing her best traits as her worst faults! No thank you.

Anyway, it was time to go home and consume a crate of brownies or something else decadently chocolate. Maybe on her way back to the Big Sky B and B, she'd think of a suitable bribe to get her sister in the kitchen, and baking.

Cleo drove down the winding country road, appreciating late spring in Montana and watching eagerly for her first soothing glimpse of Blue Mirror Lake. Yes, the B and B was a sensible, practical place for her to live, but it was a choice she didn't regret. She'd like to travel, sure, but this piece of Montana and the lake would always be home. She was glad her mother had convinced her father to leave Louisiana and open the business all those years ago.

Thinking of Louisiana reminded Cleo of her mother's nightmares. There. Another reason that living at the bed-and-breakfast was a good choice. She wanted to be near Celeste while these terrible dreams continued to plague her.

What the heck were they all about? Cleo pursed her lips and vowed to sit her mother down for a little heart-to-heart this evening. She could picture Celeste already, her eyes shadowed and her manner subdued, as it always was the day after the dream.

Cleo parked her Volvo sedan in its usual spot and let herself inside the back door. The kitchen was immaculate, but Cleo sniffed hopefully, wondering if Jasmine had done any particularly delectable culinary experimenting that day.

A soft, delighted laugh froze her midsniff.

It was followed by another. Her mother's laugh. And then came a giggle. A baby's giggle.

Cleo gritted her teeth, a terrible premonition overcoming her. With quick steps she passed through the kitchen and dining room to the living room.

Her mother sat on one of the long couches, cradling an adorable blond, blue-eyed baby. A man, golden-haired and devastating in a dark suit, watched them from a spot by the windows.

Cleo frowned at him. For all her sniffing, it was quite a surprise she hadn't smelled a rat.

She tapped her toe against the honey-pine floor. "You're not staying *here* are you?" she asked, her voice cool, she hoped, and not crabby.

Ethan's head came up and so did his eyebrows.

Her mother smiled at the baby but addressed Cleo. "Ethan and Jonah have rented the Atchinson house."

The Atchinson house. Oh, great. Another lakeside property not more than half a mile away. She crossed her arms over her chest. "So if you have your own place, what are you doing here?"

Her mother spoke again. "Ethan came to introduce me to Jonah. And I'm thrilled to meet this very handsome young man." Celeste nuzzled the baby's cheek and the little boy giggled again, his hands patting her hair.

Cleo softened a little. Her mother looked happier than she had in a long time, and obviously distracted from the terror of the night before.

Then Ethan spoke for the first time. "And I came to see if I could persuade you to go to dinner with me at the country club."

Cleo took a step back. Oh, no. That wouldn't be sensible *or* practical. Not when he was looking like the Golden God of Business in that Italian suit. Not when the last time they'd had dinner at the country club the evening had ended with her half dressed and nearly begging him for more.

"No," she said firmly, and then smiled to herself. Sometimes sensible and practical felt darn good.

"Please, Cleo," Ethan said quietly. "It might be the last time we ever meet."

Cleo's heart jumped. The last time. But then she narrowed her eyes, staring at him suspiciously. He didn't look like a man who thought they would never meet again.

"Go ahead, sweetie," her mother added. "I told Ethan I'd watch Jonah, and I can't think of *anything* that would make me happier than watching this little angel."

Cleo softened again. Her mother *did* look so darn happy holding that baby. To be honest, she itched to hold him herself. Without even thinking about it, she walked forward and sat beside her mother on the couch, then reached out toward Jonah. He immediately grabbed her hand and gave her a grin that made mush of everything inside her.

"Please come with me, Cleo," Ethan said.

Looking at the motherless baby and sharing the joy her own mother had in just touching him, Cleo discovered her backbone had dissolved completely. She sighed and stroked Jonah's cheek with her free hand.

"All right," she said grudgingly. "This last time." Because, anyway, could she really resist just one last time with Ethan? "I need a few minutes to change."

He nodded. "Take all the time you need."

In her room, Cleo whipped through a refreshing shower and then stood in her underwear, staring into her closet. What did a woman wear for a last dinner with the man she'd refused to marry? The man who considered her so practical and sensible?

The answer was obvious, of course. A woman should wear something completely impractical and as far from sensible as possible. Something that would make him sweat and make him drool.

But Cleo being Cleo, she had nothing remotely close to that in her closet.

She went wild, double-checking, flinging hangers aside with abandon until she had to admit the closest thing to "vamp" in her closet was the black witch's costume she wore at Beansprouts on Halloween. And even that was something that had been Jasmine's first.

"Jasmine," Cleo whispered. Her mother had said her sister was out for the evening, but Cleo dashed through their adjoining bathroom into her room, anyway. Without a moment's compunction, she went double-fast through her sister's double-stuffed closet and emerged clutching a long-sleeved black knit dress that was deeply veed in the front and back.

Not allowing herself to give in to doubt, she ran back to her own room and slipped into black stockings, black heels, and the dynamite black dress that had been bought by her less-curvy sister. Sitting at her dressing table, she twisted her wavy hair behind her head and held it back with a jeweled comb. Then she applied her makeup heavier than usual, not daring to look past her chin.

Once she'd blotted her lipstick, a shade named Derring Do, Cleo stood. With a deep breath, she turned around and looked at herself in the full-length mirror.

"Eek," she said breathlessly. Where the dress had displayed a lot of Jasmine's fragile clavicle and just a hint of her bust, on Cleo, the dress displayed a lot of bust and nothing, but *nothing* was hinted at. "Oh, boy," she whispered.

Could she do it? With fingers that trembled just a little, she pulled a couple of wavy tendrils free from the twist of her hair, letting them drift softly around her face. Could she walk out there and face Ethan in something so…well, sophisticated instead of sensible?

Taking a deep breath—and then swearing to herself to not take another after what she noticed it did to her cleavage—Cleo gave herself one more objective, assessing look in the mirror.

And liked what she saw.

She strutted a couple of steps in her high heels, then made an about-face and walked past the mirror again. Yes, she thought. I'm going through with it.

Because she'd be darned if she was going to send Ethan out of her life with him remembering a boringly sensible, practical, capable Cleo. And if this dress didn't make him look at her just a teensy bit differently, then her name wasn't Cleo Kincaid Monroe.

By the time they'd left the B and B, settled into his Range Rover and driven to the Whitehorn Country Club, Cleo was pretty sure that Ethan didn't know *what* to think when he looked at her. While her mother had smiled and told Cleo how nice she looked, Ethan appeared to have swallowed his tongue. The miles to the country club had been covered in virtual silence and Cleo got the distinct feeling that Ethan was glad to have something to focus on besides her and the dress she was wearing.

Which was why she smiled at him smugly as he took his seat across from her at their intimate table for two. She didn't need to be embarrassed about the marriage proposal any longer. Ethan could now see that she was a woman who didn't have to resort to convenient marriages.

She figured that was what he was coming to grips with as they gave the waiter their orders and were served a bottle of excellent wine. Ethan was terse, a fact that made Cleo even more warm and gracious.

Once they were finally alone, Cleo held up her wineglass, watching the golden wine glow in the soft candlelight. "What should we drink to?" she said lightly.

Regrets came to mind. The kind of regrets she hoped he had for underestimating her qualities. Of course, he might suggest they drink to her beauty—no, her sexiness, she thought, wiggling in her seat. Drinking to her sexiness would be just right.

Ethan suddenly closed his eyes, opened them. "To my apologies," he said tersely.

Cleo blinked. Okay. Fine. Apologies would work. There was regret in apologies, though no acknowledgment of sexiness, darn him. But apologies certainly meant Ethan realized she wasn't the type of woman to leap on a man's proposal when all he wanted from her was her capability.

She shrugged and clinked her glass against the rim of his. The first sip of the delicious wine was slipping over her tongue when he continued.

"My apologies for not presenting my proposal in a more businesslike way," he said. "I wasn't thinking clearly earlier. Blame it on the mess my life is in."

Cleo held on to that mouthful of wine, uncertain she remembered how to swallow. He was apologizing for not proposing in a *more* businesslike way?

He sighed. "I didn't present any reasons *you* might be interested in the deal—I mean, marriage. But let me assure you I've thought that through now." With a flick of his wrist, he downed the contents of his glass in one gulp. "First, let me assure you that the physical aspect of our merger—uh, marriage—needn't happen until and unless you're ready."

The wine still in her mouth, Cleo blinked. He was just shrugging off the idea of making love with her—until! he'd said, unless!—when she was wearing the most sophisticated, most sexy dress she'd ever worn in her life.

He must have taken her silence as a prompt to go on, because he now looked her full in the face. "And, Cleo, second, and best of all…" He paused a moment, deal-making charisma oozing off him. "If you marry me, I'll buy the Beansprouts's building and list the deed in your name."

That's when Cleo finally tried to swallow, quickly, so she could get right to telling him what she thought of such a businesslike…bribe. Yes. That's what it was, all right, a bribe. But either the wine went down the wrong way or her throat was as angry as the rest of her and forgot to actually accept the liquid.

In any case, instead of telling Ethan off, Cleo found herself fighting for breath. She choked and coughed, thinking she might die from lack of oxygen, instead of at the hands of the state, a much more predictable fate considering what she felt like doing to Ethan.

"Cleo! Are you all right?"

Her napkin to her mouth, she looked up, into the concerned face of John Riker. His wife, Rosemary, bustled over and started patting Cleo briskly on the back.

Thanks to Rosemary and a couple of sips of water, Cleo managed to catch her breath and then smile at her longtime friends. "I haven't seen you two in ages," she said, her voice only a little hoarse from all the coughing.

She stood to hug Rosemary, and then turned to John. A sweet smile transformed his craggy face to something just this side of beautiful. He took her hands in his huge ones. "Cleo, my love." His arms came around her and he swept her up for a bearlike squeeze.

Cleo giggled. Embracing John was like embracing one of the ageless pines surrounding Blue Mirror Lake. He was as dear as he was sturdy. With an appreciative smack, he kissed her on the lips.

From the other side of the table came the sound of an ominously cleared throat. Cleo ignored it. Ignored him. Ethan. She still couldn't believe he would so cold-bloodedly frame his second proposal of marriage, and she needed a little time to decide exactly how she was going to tell him no, no way, no how.

But he cleared his throat again, and John set her on her feet. "Won't you introduce us?" John asked in his booming voice.

Cleo sighed, but turned toward Ethan. His eyes looked kind of glittery and he was staring at John. "Rosemary and John Riker, this is an…acquaintance of mine, Ethan Redford."

He stood as she spoke and came around the table to shake first Rosemary's, then John's hand. "I'm a friend of Cleo's," he corrected. "A close friend." His palm came to rest on her shoulder.

Cleo ignored the heat running down her arm. "I've known John since we were kids."

John teasingly tugged one of the tendrils of hair around her face. "But you sure look all grown up tonight."

As if Ethan even noticed it, darn him. Cleo pushed lightly against John's shoulder. "Flatterer," she said fondly.

Ethan's fingers squeezed her shoulder. "Don't let us hold you up."

Cleo turned her head to look at him. His face was a perfect mask of politeness, but she could feel the tension in his body. Of course, he'd just asked her to marry him and she'd yet to give him her answer. She liked the idea he might be a little anxious about it.

She smiled gaily at Rosemary and John. "Please say you can join us. It would be *so* much more fun as a foursome." Cleo ignored a second squeeze from Ethan's hand.

Rosemary cocked an eyebrow and darted a look at Ethan. "Oh, I don't know…"

But John didn't need to be asked twice. "For a drink, Rosie. Then we'll get our own table. I want to know what Cleo's been up to." He chuckled. "And who she's been up to it with."

Rosemary rolled her eyes. "John."

Cleo just whacked him with another light punch and grinned. She didn't mind John's teasing if it meant Ethan would have to squirm for a while.

Once they were all seated at the table and the other couple's drinks served, John leaned back and gave Cleo another once-over. "Have I mentioned you look like a million bucks? You're going to break my heart a second time, I swear."

Cleo grinned. "I may take you back just for the compliments."

Ethan's chair made a loud *crrrck* as he scraped it closer to the table.

Rosemary smiled and put her hand on her husband's massive forearm. "You're making Cleo's date nervous, John, with all this talk." She turned toward Ethan. "Cleo and John were an item once upon a time. She was the best thing that ever happened to him."

John grinned. "Until she tore my heart out of my chest and stomped all over it."

It was Cleo's turn to roll her eyes. "We were in college, John. You loved beer more than you ever loved me, admit it."

John's grin died. "Nah, Cleo, honey, I really loved you." But the light in his eyes was for his wife when he turned his gaze to her. "But then I met Rosemary."

Cleo smiled, remembering, and sent a significant

look Ethan's way. "Whom *I* introduced him to, by the way."

"How…fortunate for all three of you," he said. He wore that deal-maker's poker face of his. "How long ago did you say this was?" he addressed this last to Rosemary.

She sipped at her glass of red wine. "Hmm. Five years ago? We've been married for two."

"That's right," Cleo said. "You were married the same week I opened Beansprouts."

"A business that certainly deserves to remain open," Ethan murmured. Beneath the table, he touched her hand. He linked his fingers with hers and held on tight when she instantly tried to pull away.

Rosemary smiled, unaware of the undertones beneath Ethan's compliment. "Cleo does wonders with the business *and* the children."

"Always knew she'd make a success of it," John added. "Cleo is a detail person."

"Hey, come on, you guys." Cleo squirmed in her seat, embarrassed.

"Now you shush," Rosemary answered. "There's no reason we can't tell Ethan about you."

Cleo groaned, feeling pretty certain that for some reason her friends had decided to foster the romance they supposed—oh, so wrongly—was going on between her and Ethan.

"I'd like to know everything about Cleo," Ethan said smoothly. "Please go on."

Cleo groaned again. The only thing he needed to know was how quickly she could spit out the letters n-o. "Really, guys—"

"She's the most sensible woman I know."

Rosemary's obviously heartfelt words penetrated Cleo like a blade. *Sensible?* She stared at her friend. Is that how Rosemary saw her, too?

"Why I remember a time in college when the rest of us were gung-ho for a road trip to San Francisco. While we were throwing stuff in backpacks and arguing about how to divvy up the driving, it was Cleo who checked the road conditions, called the weather service, and determined that not only was our car without a first-aid kit, it didn't have a spare tire, either." Rosemary smiled. "And you were right, Cleo. We should have listened to you. We ran into a storm two hours out and had a flat six hours after that."

"And I bet Cleo was the only one who knew how to change a tire," Ethan said.

A chill ran down Cleo's back. "I didn't go," she said slowly. "I had an early class on the day they were planning to get back and I was worried about missing it."

Rosemary beamed. "What did I tell you? Always sensible."

Cleo swallowed. "But, remember? You had a

terrific time. You brought me back one of those little cable cars from a souvenir shop. I keep it at Beansprouts." Now that she thought about it, she didn't know what made her give it that place of honor on her desk. To remind her of what? That she'd never seen San Francisco because she'd made the wise, sensible choice?

"Don't pout, honey," John said teasingly. "If we all followed our bliss who would be around to mop up the mess we left behind? We need you practical, capable types."

Cleo hid behind her glass of wine. *If we all followed our bliss*...John did that. He'd taken the same business courses she had and ended up with his own successful enterprise—he made a fortune in woodworking, crafting unique custom cabinetry and such with his own two hands. His bliss.

Conversation continued around the table and Cleo let it go on without her. John said they needed the practical, capable types. Like her.

Was she this sturdy old stick that everyone saw her as? Sure she loved Beansprouts and was happy working at her business, but when she thought of following her bliss...

She slid her gaze toward Ethan. And like that, she remembered his kiss, the sensation of his palms cupping her face, the catch in his voice when he peeled her dress from her shoulders....

Her fingers tightened on the stem of her wineglass and she tugged on her other fingers, the ones Ethan still claimed. Without a pause in what he was saying to John and Rosemary, he held on.

Cleo swallowed, her gaze following his handsome profile. *Bliss.*

"Are you okay?" Rosemary's voice snuck under the louder conversation of the men.

Cleo swallowed again. "I'm...not sure." Which even to her own ears sounded odd. She was always sure about things. Sensible, safe choices. Practical decisions.

"He's to die for," Rosemary whispered, her gaze flicking toward Ethan. "And when I saw the way he looks at you and the way you look at him...whoa!"

Cleo raised her eyebrows and thought maybe her friend should consider another line of work. Rosemary was an artist, which should have made her an excellent observer, but though Cleo might be guilty of going moony over Ethan, the reverse was definitely not true. He saw her as a sensible-practical-capable person.

Not as a to-drool-for woman.

Anyway, people shouldn't marry someone they think of as practical and capable any more than someone should marry over a little lust.

"He has a child," she told Rosemary suddenly. "A baby. His sister died and he has custody of his nephew." The thought of Jonah's blond chubbiness made her stomach clench. And then clench harder, when she thought of the hard, golden man who cared enough about his dead sister and her child to do anything to keep him close.

"Like your mother and Summer," Rosemary said softly.

Cleo nodded. Like her mother and Summer... When Cleo's aunt Blanche died, before Cleo was even born, Yvette and Celeste had raised Blanche's daughter Summer. Yvette looked after her while Celeste was in Louisiana, but when Celeste returned and Yvette married and moved to the house behind the B and B, Summer had continued to live with Celeste. Summer, Cleo and Jasmine, and their cousin Frannie had been raised as sisters, loved each other as sisters.

That was what Ethan wanted for Jonah. Love and family.

"I—" she broke off and looked desperately at Rosemary as a scary, life-altering realization crystallized in her mind. "Marriage is forever, isn't it?"

Rosemary smiled softly. "It doesn't seem that long when you're in love with the person you're married to."

In love.

Cleo gripped her wineglass again. "Rosemary, talk me out of something. Tell me to think sensibly. Tell me to be practical."

Rosemary's smile widened. "Are you talking to

me? I went to San Francisco, remember? I'm an artist."

"You follow your bliss."

Rosemary nodded. "Always, Cleo. And if I take a wrong path or two, well the bliss more than makes up for it."

Oh, God. Cleo wished Rosemary hadn't said that. But though she could wish the whole conversation away, could wish they'd never run into Rosemary and John, none of the wishing would change the truth.

Cleo met her bliss the day she met Ethan Redford. She'd fallen in love with him that instant, as improbable and impractical as it sounded.

And sensible, capable Cleo just couldn't deny it any longer. Maybe she didn't want to. Maybe at twenty-seven years old it was time to damn the consequences and embrace her bliss.

Embrace Ethan.

A delighted, thrilled shiver wiggled down her spine. She squeezed Ethan's hand and he stopped talking to John and gave her a questioning look.

Cleo took a deep breath. There would be time to make him drool later. "Why don't we go ahead and tell them?" she said.

Ethan stilled and his eyes widened. Oh, they were so heartbreakingly blue. "You mean…?"

She nodded and then tried smiling, but she wasn't sure how it came off when she knew there was more than a hint of tears in her eyes. "John, Rosemary. Ethan and I are going to be married."

Around the table, she noted varied reactions. Rosemary wore an expression of gentle delight. John was out-and-out grinning, which told Cleo that somehow Ethan had worked his deal-maker magic and already made a buddy.

As for Ethan himself…he didn't look at all surprised that the sensible woman he'd asked to marry him had made such a practical decision as to commit to a man who offered brick-and-mortar buildings instead of tender emotion.

She sighed, letting the reality of what she'd just done wash over her. She, practical, sensible Cleo Monroe, loved Ethan Redford. There was no question about that.

But would she ever be capable of getting Ethan to love her back?

Four

The next evening the doorbell rang at Ethan's rented house. Seated in the deep, comfortable couch, he threw down the report he'd been reading.

"That's her," he told his nephew. Jonah sat in a hammock-like baby chair on the coffee table in front of the couch. "It's Cleo."

The baby blinked, and then rolled his eyes in the direction of the striking view of Blue Mirror Lake from the room's huge picture window. Ethan followed his gaze, then stared at the French doors leading to the spacious deck—the last possible escape route before he made what could be the biggest mistake of his life.

"I wanted a mother figure, bud," he whispered to the baby. But instead, the certainly attractive, yet maternal Cleo of his memory had turned into a tantalizing siren last night. Oh, he'd known she had that side to her, too—it wasn't as if he'd forgotten the time he'd kissed her mouth and touched her luscious skin—but he'd thought he could focus on her mothering qualities.

Well, hell, not in that piece of shrink-wrap she'd called a dress last night. He'd barely kept his hands to himself and then his irritation under control when another man's hands—those of her old boyfriend John—had so naturally touched her.

The doorbell rang again. With a sigh, Ethan stood. It wasn't as if he had any choice. He'd proposed, she'd accepted, and then they'd calmly discussed their future plans. Plans that included getting Jonah accustomed to her as soon as possible. Hence tonight's dinner.

He pulled open the door just as Cleo rang the bell once more. He hoped the echoing sound would account for the stupid expression he figured took over his face, because even in a casual pair of jeans and a lightweight apricot-colored turtleneck, she made his blood chug hotly through his veins, just as she had the night before in the slinky dress.

"Hi." Cleo held out a bottle of wine and smiled.

Chug-a-chug-chug went his blood, pulsing a slow burn through his body. Hell. Ethan set his jaw. How terrible would it be if he grabbed the wine but then shut the door on her pretty, tempting face?

Cleo stepped closer and lifted the bottle she held

higher. "Jasmine said this would go well with the meal you conned her into making us."

Ethan found his voice. "I wanted the meal to be something special." That was before he'd been having these doubts. Really, it wasn't too late to call the whole thing off. Some other woman, some woman who looked less like something he wanted to savor for dessert and more like a Mrs. Cleaver mother-type who would *make* desserts, would be better. Safer.

If this marriage—if Ethan himself—took the sparkle out of Cleo's wide violet eyes, he'd never be able to look himself in the face again. "Cleo—"

But her gaze drifted past him and her face changed, her mouth softening. "Oh," she said softly. "There he is." The wine was thrust against his chest and he caught it as she brushed by him and headed for Jonah.

Something contracted painfully inside the emptiness in Ethan's chest. There had been tears in Cleo's eyes. He closed his, damn grateful. No matter what risks, Jonah deserved a woman who cried the first time she saw him after agreeing to be his mother.

Ethan shut the door and turned to see Cleo pluck the baby from his chair. She held him up, so they were nearly nose to nose, and Jonah gave her that hopeful don't-I-know-you smile of his that never failed to stab Ethan. It seemed to be the smile of a baby who was desperately looking for his place in the world.

Cleo fussed over Jonah, praising his intelligence, size and beauty. The baby listened avidly to each soft word and his hands reached out for Cleo's face. She cuddled him against her chest.

Ethan swallowed. "Can I get you something? A drink?"

Cleo didn't take her gaze off the baby. "How about a glass of the wine I brought and some directions?"

"Directions?"

She flicked a glance Ethan's way. The sparkle was there, bright as Christmas lights. "To the diaper changing area. I think this guy could use my services."

Ethan pointed her down the hallway to the baby's bedroom, then poured a glass of wine for each of them. He trailed her to Jonah's room, following the sound of more feminine nonsense talk. Her diaper-changing skills were a lot more professional than his first efforts had been.

"You're good," he said admiringly. "When I first started changing Jonah I had pangs of guilt over my contribution to the landfill problem. About one in four diapers actually stayed on him."

The fresh diaper fastened, Cleo leaned down to kiss the baby's tummy. Jonah kicked in delight, and Ethan thought about her lips on *his* body… Anywhere close to his stomach would do.

She looked over at Ethan and he quickly schooled his features. "We should consider using cloth diapers for that very reason," she said. "Do you have any objections?" With a few efficient movements she redressed the baby.

"No objections at all, but I don't want to make too much work for you," he answered.

Cleo lifted the baby off the changing table and against her shoulder again. "I'd like to raise him, even from the beginning, with a concern for the environment."

Ethan just nodded, his mind not going past "I'd like to raise him." His pulse did that *chug-a-chug* again, but this time the heat was accompanied with a sweet feeling of relief. He'd found someone to raise Jonah. He'd feared all along that he didn't have what it took to nurture a child to adulthood. No good example to follow, no notion of how to figure it all out.

But Cleo. Cleo would know what to do.

Even if he failed her, she wouldn't fail Jonah.

She was looking at him strangely, so he tried to put a smile on his face. "What about dinner? Are you ready?"

"Sure," she said. "Show me how I can help."

In the kitchen, she bustled around, finding plates and silverware to set the table. Ethan was nonplussed again. When he was caring for the baby, he never was quite sure what to *do* with him. Well, Cleo did everything with Jonah. She managed to accomplish her tasks with the baby sort of balanced on her hip, and Jonah appeared enthralled by all the movement and the constantly changing sights.

For his part, Ethan felt pretty lame as all he did was fill their plates with what Jasmine had prepared. When everything was on the table, Cleo sat with Jonah still in her arms.

"Let me take him," Ethan said. "Or I can put him in his baby chair. He's not much of a complainer."

Cleo shook her head. "Do you mind if I keep him close?"

"How are you going to eat?"

"I'll manage." She smiled. "It's more important that Jonah gets used to me than I clean my plate."

Another wave of thankfulness rushed over Ethan. She was putting Jonah first. That was what the baby needed and deserved. If he just concentrated on that, maybe he could ignore the desire he felt for Cleo. The entanglements of sex and need might lead them straight to disaster. He wasn't going to risk Jonah's welfare for a few hot times in the sheets.

He cleared his throat and toyed with his salad. "Jasmine said you told your family we're getting married." But Cleo's sister hadn't spilled a hint of what their reaction had been.

Cleo's expression didn't give anything away,

either. Despite Jonah, she'd managed a mouthful of Jasmine's chicken and she nodded as she chewed.

Ethan cleared his throat again. "So, um, what did they think?"

Cleo shrugged. "They're my family. They like you. They respect my decisions and will always be behind me."

Family was what he wanted for Jonah. And he felt certain that all of Cleo's family would take the little boy to their hearts. "Is next week still okay for the wedding?" That was what they'd decided last night.

Cleo's cheeks flushed, but she nodded. "Just fine. Friday, right?"

"Friday. And then I thought we could live here, at least for a few months. I have it leased through the summer. After that we can find something else."

Cleo looked down at Jonah and made funny faces at him. "This is really going to happen, isn't it?" she said softly. "I'm going to have a son…and a husband."

"Cleo, look at me." He waited for her gaze to meet his. "I'm not playing. Next Friday, if you're sure, we'll get married. It will really happen."

Her eyes were so incredibly violet and so wide that he would find it much too easy to be mesmerized by them. But he had promises to make before those wedding vows. "I want us to marry." He really did, he realized.

For Jonah's sake.

"And I'm going to do my damned best not to screw it up. I've got to be honest, I've never wanted to be married and I've never wanted to have a child. But that's in the past. Now I'm committed to providing for you and Jonah. I work hard and I make good money. Better than good. And every dollar I have will be yours and Jonah's."

Two worry lines appeared between Cleo's brows. "This is not about money, Ethan."

"It's what I have to offer, Cleo." All he had to offer. "And speaking of business, don't forget that Jonah and I have to head back to Houston tomorrow evening."

Those worry lines continued to mar the smooth skin of her forehead. "About that…I was wondering if you'd leave Jonah with me. I'm planning on going part-time at Beansprouts for a few weeks and doing a lot of my administrative tasks from home. Jonah would work right into that."

Ethan frowned. "Oh, I don't think so. The nanny in Houston said she'd be available."

"I'll take good care of him."

"It's not that, it's—" It was that Ethan couldn't imagine coming home at night to his Houston condo and finding it empty. "Let me think about it."

Jonah, tiring of sitting in one place, distracted their attention. Ethan welcomed the new focus, though it meant more opportunity to notice how very natural Cleo was with the baby—so much more natural than he had ever been. He turned on the stereo, having at least discovered that the baby enjoyed country music, and it made him feel…something he couldn't quite name when he watched Cleo two-step around the kitchen with Jonah in her arms.

"We should go dancing sometime," Ethan said suddenly.

Cleo's feet stopped their cute little shuffle. She looked at him, all wide-eyed again, and Ethan wondered what it would be like to hold her curvy body against his chest and to have that remarkable hair tickling his chin. He remembered the sweet scent of it, and his blood *chug-a-chug-chugged* toward his groin.

She licked her lips, and Ethan almost groaned. "I'd like that," she said. "Very much."

Damn. He wasn't supposed to be thinking of her lips, her curves, or her scent. No embracing. No dancing. Because if he got too close to Cleo and their romantic relationship went sour, where would that leave Jonah?

He turned away from her. "Yeah, well, sometime. Maybe," he said, his voice gruff.

Hers was carefully neutral. "Would you mind if I gave Jonah his bath?"

"No problem. I'll just finish the dishes."

Which only took a few minutes. Yet by the time he'd put them away and wandered toward Jonah's bathroom, Cleo had the baby's safety seat in the warm water and Jonah already in it. She was singing something about a spider as she gently washed him.

The baby's gaze was glued to her face. Ethan leaned against the doorjamb and watched the picture they made, feeling as if he'd wandered into someone else's life. It all seemed so normal and natural, so much the way it should be, but so much what he didn't know about.

He wanted to reach out to stroke Cleo's hair, and then Jonah's pink, just-washed skin, but it was as if a glass wall had been erected between the door and the bathtub.

"Are you okay?" Cleo looked over her shoulder at him, her face flushed from the warmth of the water.

Ethan's mind instantly conjured up an image of Cleo, pink and glistening from her bath. He imagined himself washing her, touching those beautiful breasts, his soapy hands running along the curves of her hips.

Her nostrils flared. "Ethan?"

He shook himself out of the fantasy, afraid she might read his thoughts. "Hmm?" Even his "hmm" sounded hoarse.

"What were you thinking about?" Her voice sounded a little hoarse, too.

He swallowed. "About tomorrow," he lied. "I

think it will be fine if Jonah stays with you while I'm on this trip to Houston." There really had never been any doubt. He wanted the baby to become accustomed to Cleo—the mother Ethan had brought into Jonah's life.

Of course there were no guarantees that Ethan himself would ever become accustomed to Cleo. And if the fantasies he'd been indulging in and the hardened state of his body were any indication, the resounding answer was no.

It was one thing to say you were going to do something impractical for once, Cleo thought, and an entirely other thing to actually *do* it.

In the kitchen at Ethan's—no, *their*—house, she stared down at the brand-new platinum-and-diamond wedding band on her fourth finger. She'd married Ethan Redford three hours before. Jonah—her son—was asleep for the night in his bedroom. He'd gone down like a dream, wearing a teeny smile that she pretended was because he understood they'd created a family for him today.

The one thing that had been easy about this whole situation was caring for Jonah. She'd fallen for him almost as quickly as she'd fallen for his uncle. At first it was because a motherless baby was a certain draw to her maternal heart.

But then, quickly, it was for Jonah himself. Because he was a morning person, as she was.

Because of the way he snuggled his head into the hollow of her shoulder. Because his smiles beamed at her now with a confidence and familiarity she was sure wasn't there the week before, when she'd first started caring for him full-time.

A light rap on the back door of the kitchen startled Cleo. She looked over to see Jasmine, illuminated by the small porch light, peeking through the curtains that swagged across the glassed upper half of the door. Cleo quickly crossed to turn the knob, but instead of stepping over the threshold, Jasmine merely handed over a brown grocery bag that was mouth-wateringly fragrant.

"Here," she whispered. "Take this."

Cleo looked inside and spied Jasmine's famous cashew chicken and steamed rice in clear-topped containers. "Yum, but—"

"Shh." Jasmine's eyes widened and she kept her voice hushed. "It's dinner. I thought you might need fortification or—" she giggled lightly "—inspiration."

Cleo's cheeks went warm but she ignored her sister's teasing. "Excuse me, but why exactly are we whispering?"

"So you can tell Ethan you just whipped it up yourself. You said he hadn't had a chance to eat any of your cooking yet, and I thought—"

Cleo groaned. "Jasmine, sooner or later the man's going to have to find out I'm cuisinely clueless."

She'd only been able to postpone the inevitable because Ethan had been out of town since the day after they'd last eaten one of Jasmine's meals. Cleo had lived at the house with Jonah all week, but Ethan had only arrived back early that afternoon, just in time for their four o'clock wedding.

She bit her lip. "He's exhausted and I said I'd make us a light dinner. You don't think I'll mess up sandwiches and soup, do you?"

Jasmine rolled her eyes. "Just tell me this. Has the marriage been consummated yet?"

"Jasmine!" Cleo's face turned even hotter and she inspected a nearby pristine countertop. "I just put the baby to bed."

"Well, you better get yourself and Ethan there, as well—before you do any cooking."

"Jasmine," Cleo muttered again.

"Hey." Jasmine grinned. "A sister has to tell it like it is. Get him in the sack before you give him any of your soup and sandwiches. Otherwise, go with the good stuff." She nodded toward the bag. "'Bye!"

"'Bye," Cleo echoed faintly, but then her sister turned around. Cleo raised a brow. "What? More advice?"

Jasmine smiled. "Just a thumbs-up. Ethan's *gorgeous*. If you hadn't seen him first…"

Cleo shook her head. "Ethan's too old for you, baby sister."

"Uh-uh." Jasmine backed into the twilight. "The

males my age are boys. I want a man like Ethan, and I want my man to look at me the way Ethan looks at you." She turned and melted away into the darkness.

Cleo frowned. Great. Gone before she could pin down exactly what that "way" was. She set the bag of food on the counter and rubbed her midsection. Just hearing the words "Ethan" and "bed" in the same sentence had her stomach hiccuping again.

What way *had* he looked at her? Jasmine and Cleo's mother, cousins, aunt and uncle had all been witnesses to their civil ceremony. To her eyes, Ethan had appeared preoccupied when not downright tired. The kiss he'd brushed across her lips at the conclusion of the ceremony had less emotion than the one Uncle Edward had pressed against her cheek.

He'd seemed relieved that she'd told her family they'd save the celebrating for another day. Cleo had broken the news to them six days before, when Ethan told her he had to make an immediate and unscheduled trip to Japan, though he swore he'd make it home in time for the wedding ceremony.

Tonight would be quiet, just the three of them. Well, two actually, with the baby already asleep.

Leaving them to discuss the bed issue uninterrupted—the issue being that Cleo didn't know which one to choose tonight.

For the past week she'd been in the guest bedroom across from Jonah's room. But there was the stately master suite just down the hall, with the echoes of Ethan's spicy scent and the huge bed made for a man and a woman's...uh, comfort.

Her stomach hopped up and down again and Cleo closed her eyes. Ethan had said the physical side of their marriage would be up to her. Well, it was pretty stupid to pretend the idea of making love with him was something she even needed to consider.

She wanted to make love to him.

She wanted Ethan.

But how to broach the subject? With a frown, she swung around to look out the window over the sink and caught sight of her reflection, clear against the night's darkness. Dang, if every nervous, anxious, but aroused thought wasn't written all over her face.

Once he saw her, he'd know.

With a deep breath Cleo started across the gleaming kitchen floor. Find Ethan, she thought. Then he'd take care of the rest.

With cold fingers, she pushed through the swinging door. The faint sounds of country music came from the direction of Ethan's office at the far end of the house. She smiled to herself, remembering he said they should go dancing sometime. Maybe tonight they could begin that way, a little slow dance in each other's arms before a long, delicious night of lovemaking.

"Ethan?" she called softly, but her voice was

so squeaky she had to swallow and start over.
"Ethan?"

To give him fair warning she made her steps distinct and firm. "Ethan?" she said again.

Still no answer.

She peeked through the office doorway. His desk
was in one corner of the room and a leather couch,
its back to the entry, faced a small fire crackling in
the brick-and-stone fireplace. Clint Black sang softly
to the empty room.

Cleo shifted, anticipation building unmercilessly.
At this rate, by the time she found him, one touch
would shatter her into a zillion nervous pieces.
Clint stopped singing, and there was a brief segue
of silence before the next song on the CD began.
That was when Cleo heard it.

A sigh. No, a breath. Another one. Rhythmic
breathing.

With a sinking heart, she walked up to the couch
and peered over its high back.

Oh, there he was. Ethan. Tie loosened, ankles
crossed, gold stubble starting to bristle along his
square chin. Her bridegroom. So asleep, Cleo
guessed a marching band wouldn't wake him.

A nervous bride certainly wouldn't do it.

Would she?

She cleared her throat.

She cleared it again. Loudly.

Ethan didn't stir.

She stomped over to the fireplace and poked at the small fire until a satisfying shower of sparks hissed in the grate. Over her shoulder, Ethan continued to sleep soundly. She poked again. More sparks. More rhythmic breathing from the man on the couch.

Sighing in defeat, she walked around the end of the couch and plucked an afghan off the plump bolster by his feet. She tossed it over him, and even when the crocheted corner smacked him lightly in the nose, he didn't move. Sighing louder, she folded the offending—and useless—corner back from his face.

She slipped his loafers off his feet, letting them fall to the floor with noisy clunks. When he still didn't rouse, she turned out the lights and turned off Clint Black.

Standing in the firelit darkness, staring down at the man who she wanted naked and next to her more than anything else, she considered herself one of the most understanding—frustrated—women in the world.

With Jonah perched on one hip, Cleo sipped a fresh mug of her sister's awesome coffee. Jasmine stood nearby, chopping walnuts for the waffles she was serving that morning to the B and B guests. "What are we going to do about Mama?" Cleo asked her sister. Upon arriving at the bed-and-breakfast earlier, she'd discovered Celeste had been up since 4:00 a.m., when another nightmare had woken her.

Jasmine shrugged. "Until she tells us more about the darned dreams, or is at least willing to tell *someone* about them, what can we do?" She looked over her shoulder and raised her eyebrows. "And to tell the truth, I'm almost just as worried about *you*. Don't you think you should be home with your husband the morning after your wedding?"

Cleo turned her gaze on Jonah and gave him a big smacking kiss on his nose. He grinned. She grinned back. "Please. Mama already fussed at me. But Ethan's exhausted from his overseas trip, and Jonah and I didn't want to disturb him, okay?"

Jasmine lips quirked up. "Exhausted, you say? That sounds promising." Her eyes narrowed. "But shouldn't you be exhausted then, too?"

Cleo shook her head. "Shut up, Jasmine."

Jasmine's gaze darted toward the dining room and she lowered her voice. "Seriously. I saw it on 'Oprah.' If you don't know what I mean, there are manuals—"

"Jasmine!" Cleo set her mug on the countertop and used her free hand to cover one of Jonah's ears. "There are children present. And I don't need any manuals, thank you very much."

Jasmine blinked. "Okay. But does Ethan?" she asked seriously.

"Does Ethan what?" a new voice asked.

Both Cleo and Jasmine whipped around, to find that the man in question had just slipped in the back door. Jonah kicked and so did Cleo's heart. Ethan had changed into jeans and a T-shirt, but he hadn't shaved and his dark gold hair stood on end. He crossed his arms over his chest. "Does Ethan what?" he asked again.

"Noth—"

"Need manuals," Jasmine said over Cleo. "L-o-v-e manuals." She wiggled her eyebrows.

The look in Ethan's eyes was unreadable as he transferred his gaze from Jasmine to Cleo. Lord, but she hoped tomato-red was her color, because her face was so hot it just had to be that particular shade. Then his gaze slid off her face, and down, down to— Oh, please, don't let her nipples be hardening from the mere brush of his gaze.

She shifted Jonah so that he covered both strategic areas. Then she tried on a sickly smile. "Sleep well?"

He drifted closer to her, picked her mug up off the counter and sipped from it. "I'm sorry," he said quietly. "I went comatose on you, didn't I?"

The back door opened again and a handsome, tanned man came in, carrying two stacked produce boxes. "Hey, ladies!" He slid the boxes onto the kitchen table. "The asparagus looks good today, Jasmine."

Then his gaze snagged on Ethan, standing so

close to Cleo. His eyes widened. "It wasn't just a rumor?" he asked, looking again at Jasmine.

"Nope, Cleo really got hitched yesterday afternoon." Jasmine performed introductions with the point of her wicked-looking butcher knife. "Ethan Redford, this is Jeremy Ricksley, our local organic farmer. Jer, this is Ethan."

Ethan held out his hand, but Jeremy ignored it to sweep Cleo—Jonah, too—into a green-smelling embrace. "I'll be damned." He released her, kissed her cheek, hugged her again, then gave her another kiss, this one on the mouth. "Congratulations."

Cleo smiled and gave his cheek a pat. Jeremy was such a dear, dear, old friend. "Thanks, sweetie," she said.

Jeremy spun in his work boots. "And you," he said to Ethan. He slapped him on the back, causing Ethan to hop forward a few inches. "You hooked the best woman in town," Jeremy said.

"Is that so," Ethan replied carefully, rotating his shoulders as if checking to see they still worked.

"Man, yes! Broke my heart a dozen times, I'll tell you, but it was worth it. She gave me the best kiss of my life."

Ethan froze. "Is that so," he said again.

Cleo rolled her eyes. "In fifth grade, Jeremy. Mention that part."

Jeremy smirked. "Okay, but that was just our *first* kiss."

Cleo rolled her eyes again. Yeah, Jeremy had caught her once beneath some mistletoe, but he'd smelled like beer and been on the rebound, so she'd quickly left him to his own devices.

"Oh, well. Fifth grade." Ethan seemed to relax a little. He even smiled.

Cleo looked at him sharply. Wait a minute. Maybe she liked it a little better when he was wondering what kind of kisses she'd exchanged with Jeremy. Ethan certainly hadn't given her any worth talking about yesterday.

He started small-talking with Jeremy, apparently now quite at ease with her elementary school conquest. Jeremy went on and on about her virtues, which would have been all right if he'd concentrated on her great kisses, Cleo thought. Maybe then Ethan would regret what hadn't happened the night before.

Instead, Jeremy was telling Ethan how business-like Cleo was. He told Ethan they served on a committee together for the local chamber of commerce. Everyone knew they could rely on Cleo. Practical, sensible Cleo.

Ugh.

Cleo sipped her coffee, tuning out the men's voices and stealing little glances at her new husband. Ethan seemed plenty rested now, all ready to be sociable. But could he have saved a little something of himself for her last night? No. When she was all hot and flustered and thinking lusty thoughts, he'd been sawing logs as though deep winter was coming.

She frowned. Then there was that smile of his when Jeremy'd mentioned fifth grade. Oh, yeah, immediately Ethan's interest in who else she'd kissed had cooled way down when he'd heard those words. Maybe he didn't think a woman as practical and capable as she could attract a *grown* man.

Cleo bit her lower lip. And maybe she couldn't. After all, she and Ethan had only had that one brief interlude of passion months ago. If it was as memorable for Ethan as it was for her, why *hadn't* he been able to stay awake last night?

A cold dousing of embarrassment ran over her. Suddenly she was thankful he hadn't woken up. He probably didn't want her *that* way. After all, he'd been willing to postpone the intimate part of their marriage indefinitely.

Another sip of Jasmine's coffee tasted bitter in her mouth. Cleo had almost made a fool of herself last night by putting the moves on him. Well, that wouldn't happen again.

Unless she was positively, absolutely, certain he did want her.

Five

Three days into his marriage, Ethan hung up the phone in the room he used as an office and sought out Cleo. He wasn't accustomed to discussing his plans with anyone, but he realized that his upcoming schedule had to be presented to his...wife.

It was still hard to think the word. Wife. He had one.

He found her in Jonah's room, standing at the changing table. Ethan hesitated in the doorway, watching her spread lotion over the baby's freshly bathed skin. Cleo was whispering something to Jonah and smiling, and he stared back at her with all the intent of a man—albeit an infant one—deeply in love.

Cleo picked up the lotion bottle and as she upended it, she glanced over her shoulder and spotted

Ethan. She froze, in the act of squeezing apparently, because a huge dollop squirted into her hand and threatened to overflow her cupped palm.

"Whoops." She hastily set the bottle down and stared at her hand in dismay. "Did you need something?"

Ethan came closer. "Sorry to startle you. Can I, uh, help?"

"Thanks." She shuffled a bit to the side. "Take the baby, will you?"

Ethan hesitated, then gamely reached for the wiggling body of his nephew. He held him awkwardly against his chest.

"Hold it right there," Cleo said. She dabbed two fingers into the lotion in her palm and rubbed the stuff into the skin of Jonah's back above his soft cloth diaper.

Ethan held the baby awkwardly and breathed in the powdery scent of the lotion. Jonah's eyes were wide as they took in his face, and guilt pinged Ethan. With expert Cleo on the scene, he left most of the baby-tending to her. He'd never quite gotten the hang of what Jonah needed.

And for his sister Della's sake, he'd been determined to find someone who could.

Hence the marriage, hence this moment, hence the uncomfortable task of sharing his life with another person. Of course, marrying Cleo had been his idea, but it still took some getting used to.

He cleared his throat. "I wanted to tell you— I mean, talk to you about my schedule for the next couple of weeks."

"Okay." Cleo dabbed her fingers into the lotion again but this time rubbed it on herself instead of the baby, her hand moving against the smooth skin of her arm.

Ethan forgot what he was supposed to be talking about. He watched her fingers make circles, circles. Then she bent and started stroking her calves with the stuff, lifting the long hem of her skirt to new heights.

His muscles tightened. Maybe he'd never before seen Cleo's knees.

Which led his thoughts instantly back to their wedding night. If he hadn't had to bust his butt getting from one side of the world to the other... If he hadn't gone to sleep on her...would those knees be something he was intimately familiar with by now?

He imagined his hands where hers were, his palms just there, on the inside of her knees. He imagined pushing them apart so he could push the part of him that was going hard this moment into her...

"Ethan?"

He shook his head to clear it. "What?" he said hoarsely.

She straightened and cocked an eyebrow. "Your schedule, you said?"

His mind whirled, trying to refocus. His schedule. Yeah. Right. He automatically handed Jonah back to her and shoved his hands into his pockets. To tell the truth, it was damn awkward accounting to Cleo. Maybe because his old man had never bothered to give Ethan's mom a why, wherefore, or the courtesy of a what-do-you-think.

Maybe it was because Ethan couldn't stop thinking about Cleo's knees.

He cleared his throat again. "We need to work out a few details."

She gently laid the baby back on the changing table and deftly started dressing him. "Okay."

"I need to head back to Houston in the next couple of days." He winced at the decisiveness in his voice. "I mean, if that's all right with you."

Cleo shrugged. "No problem."

No problem. That should be good. But instead it bothered him a little that she was so cavalier about his comings and goings. "I might have to be gone for a week."

"Fine."

"Or two," he added, an unfamiliar feeling coming to life in his gut.

"Okay."

It was a hot feeling in his gut, completely foreign to him. She didn't blink when he said he might be gone for *two weeks?* What kind of marriage did she think they were going to have?

Maybe she had counted on him being gone most of the time. There *were* all those men who couldn't wait for chances to kiss her.

But of course that was stupid. Cleo was as loyal as he was business savvy. That fire in his belly subsided. "I don't like to be gone that long," he explained, "but I want to get my business moved to Whitehorn as soon as possible."

"What?" Her attention finally garnered, she picked up the baby and turned to face him. "You're moving the business from Houston to Montana?"

He blinked. "Of course. You didn't think I was going to add out-of-town headquarters to a business that already keeps me from home, did you?"

"Oh." She fussed with the baby's wispy hair. "Of course I didn't."

But it was obvious she had. He thought of those kissing "old friends" of hers again, but dismissed the idea again. "Anyway," he said, "if I remained headquartered in Houston, it wouldn't look very convincing to Jonah's grandparents. They need to see that we've created a two-parent, stable home for him."

"Mmm." She gave a little nod. "Jonah's grandparents. That's right. This is all about that custody issue."

There was a little edge to her voice he didn't understand. "Yes," he said quietly. "And don't think I don't appreciate what you've done, Cleo."

"What I've done," she echoed.

"Taking on the baby, me…"

She gave Jonah a big kiss on the top of his head. "Taking on the baby has been a pleasure."

Ethan noticed she said nothing about taking on him.

"But since you're going to be gone so much," Cleo continued, "do you mind if I return to Beansprouts?"

She'd taken the past couple of weeks off, though yesterday she'd driven in while Jonah was napping. "Well, uh, sure," he said. "Whatever you want."

"I'll take the baby with me, of course. I can set up a portable crib in my office and I've already increased my assistant's hours. It won't be as if I'll ignore Jonah's needs."

"I didn't think for a second you'd ignore Jonah's needs," Ethan said. The only person ignoring needs was Ethan himself. The sudden need to kiss Cleo's little frown away.

He ran his hands through his hair. "Look, I know this is weird, trying to accustom ourselves to a life together, but I trust you to do the right thing, Cleo."

"Thank you. And I trust you, Ethan."

God, he wished he was so certain. This woman had gone out on a limb for him and Jonah, and he wanted to do right by her. He figured that meant slow and cool, but all he felt was this hot, quick need to bury himself inside her and know that she couldn't get away.

Only the thought that if he got close to her he might hurt her—emotionally—stopped him. He couldn't take the risk.

Because all that heat and all that quickness reminded him much too much of his father and the way he'd hurt his family. Ethan had survived by evicting emotion from his life. But that meant he didn't know how to have the kind of relationship a woman such as Cleo would want.

He sighed and stepped back. "By the way, when I'm in Houston I'll also be moving my bank accounts. I'll do it first thing, and then call to give you the numbers."

"What would I need the numbers for?"

"Because it's your money, too. I'll have the checks and debit card sent directly here, okay?"

Cleo shook her head. "You don't have to do that. I don't want your money."

"What are you talking about? Of course I have to do that." He didn't like the stubborn expression on her face. Money was what he brought to the table, damn it. If he couldn't do anything else well, he knew he could provide for them.

"It just doesn't seem…right, somehow." Cleo frowned and looked at Jonah, who appeared serious, as if he understood the adult talk.

"Hell, Cleo, what's mine is yours. We *are* married, after all."

She looked up, her violet eyes holding questions he didn't have the answers to. "Are we?"

But that answer he knew. "Yes." The little burn in his belly had fired up again and he frowned. "We're definitely married." Before he could say something stupid, he stalked off.

Entering his office, he managed to not slam the door, but he did throw himself into his chair in front of his laptop computer. Damn, damn, damn.

He'd thought he was the one who needed to get used to being married. Ha! The joke was on him, because it was Cleo who suddenly seemed the more uncomfortable.

But they *were* married. More than half of him wanted to take her to bed right now to prove that point.

But more important was Jonah and the promise Ethan had made to his sister before she died. Jonah would have the love, the nurturing, that he and Della had missed out on. That meant Ethan couldn't take a chance on messing things up with Cleo.

Cleo sat at her desk at Beansprouts, trying to ignore the calendar that reminded her of how long Ethan had been gone. She knew he regretted the necessity of leaving Whitehorn. It was the only soothing balm to the rawness of their new and to-date tense marriage.

He'd left for Houston, as physically distant as ever.

It made her nuts, because she was aware of him every moment they were together in the house. She would catch him watching her, and her skin would prickle in awareness. He would walk past her and she would follow him with her gaze, drinking in his lean strength and the graceful, male way he moved.

Though they still weren't comfortable in their marriage, he'd called her every night over the past week. No surprise, Ethan wasn't a chatterer, but the sound of his voice in her ear created a new intimacy between them. They talked of their child—that's what Cleo was careful to do, refer to him as "our boy." Ethan seemed to be getting used to it, though the first time she used the term, there had been forty-five full seconds of silence before he'd spoken.

They talked of whatever deal he was working on and Cleo would entertain him with Beansprouts reports—Bessie had recently forgiven Kenny G. and laid a big kiss on the little boy, which had sent *him* to Cleo's office in tears.

For a few minutes each night, they laughed together.

Cleo treasured the moments because they reminded her of the first time Ethan had been in Montana. Then, she'd known he saw her as a woman, not as a sensible, capable, practical caretaker for the child who had been dropped into his life.

Last night Ethan had even mentioned a gift. "Be on the lookout for its delivery tomorrow," he'd said.

Cleo had melted with tenderness. She was lying in his bed in the master suite—she would change the bedding so he would never, ever know she'd slept there—her body a warm puddle of breathlessness. "For me?"

His voice was soft, but rough, like the tongue of a cat, and she wiggled against the sheets. "For you, Cleo. Because…" He'd let the last word trail away.

Because why? Oh, how much she'd wanted to ask.

But she hadn't managed another word, and so all morning she'd wasted time looking out the window for a delivery truck, visions of lingerie or champagne or perfume or all three in her mind.

"Cleo?" Her assistant Nancy's voice sounded from the door.

Cleo straightened her spine, trying to appear businesslike, but afraid her daydreams were still written on her face. "Yes?"

"There's a package here for you."

Cleo's heart jumped. Ethan's gift? "I can't believe I missed something being delivered." Then she flushed and tried explaining why she was suddenly so interested in deliveries. "Ethan said he was sending me a present." Then her cheeks went even warmer. The last thing she needed was someone looking over her shoulder while she opened it. But knowing Nancy...

Oh, and she was right. Not only Nancy, but the three other staff members who'd managed to find the time to wander by her office as she stared at the overlarge envelope on her desk. An envelope, she noted, made from the kind of paper guaranteed to resist water as well as dynamite.

Cleo sighed, supposing she could send them all on their way. But a sisterhood developed when there was an all-woman staff. Frank opinions, unqualified support, and the right to watch someone open a present—especially one sent by a new husband!—were givens.

She tested the package's weight. Not soft enough for lingerie, not liquid enough for champagne. A book, maybe?

Nancy reached over and poked the package. "I think it's a book," she confirmed. "Poetry, do you suppose? How romantic."

"Come on! Open it!" the others urged, and Cleo used her scissors to cut across the envelope top. Then, she hesitated, suddenly remembering Jasmine's talk the other day about love manuals. How much had Ethan heard? Her heartbeat sped up. *Thump-thump-thump.* Surely he wouldn't—

Impatient, Nancy grabbed the package and shook the contents onto the desk. A stack of paperwork—sandwiched between two pieces of cardboard and held together with a thick rubber band—slid out. Instead of a card, a yellow sticky note was slapped on the front.

"For you," it said, in a masculine slash. "As promised, and thanks again." No name.

No name was necessary. Not once Cleo freed the sheaf of papers. Because the romantic gift she'd been daydreaming about wasn't really a gift at all. *Thump.* Her heart sank. *Thump.* The pages were Ethan's half of their marriage deal. *Thump.* He'd been as good as he'd promised and bought the Beansprouts building for her. Her heart settled to a slow, resigned, disappointed beat.

Thanks again.

Not surprisingly, her friends realized her disappointment and tried to cheer Cleo up by sharing the worst gifts they'd ever received from their husbands. There were some doozies—Nancy's Glen had given her a new garage door opener for their anniversary, and for her birthday, Lorna's husband of thirty-two years had recently presented her with a squishy toilet seat that played show tunes.

"Well," Nancy finally said, shepherding the other staff members out the office door, "at least it proves he knows you, Cleo. A woman like you appreciates a practical gift."

"Yes, that's right," Cleo said, sadder than ever. It seemed that everyone saw her the same way. "'Practical' me should feel happy."

But when her friends were gone, she whispered into the empty room, "But 'practical' me also feels 'capable' of wringing that man's neck."

She tamped down a sudden urge to jump up on her desk and scream to the world that she wasn't who they thought she was. She suppressed a second impulse to call Ethan and whisper scandalous things in his ear, just to shake him up.

Why couldn't people—Ethan—see that practical didn't cancel out passionate and that capable could exist alongside carnal?

Two days later Cleo waved from her office window as her mother and Jonah took off down the street. Being a grandma thrilled Celeste, and she had even bought her own stroller for her "grandbaby." She turned up her nose at the one Ethan had arrived in Montana with—it was as large and sturdy as the brand-new Range Rover he'd also purchased—but she adored touring Jonah through town in her simpler model.

Cleo relaxed against her chair. If all that her marriage gained was a new focus for her mother, something other than those disturbing dreams, then Cleo was happy.

But the soft, warm glow inside her sparked high and hot when fifteen minutes later she looked up to find her husband standing in the entry to her office.

"Ethan!" She gulped. "I didn't expect you back today."

He paused in the doorway, filling it with six plus feet of Italian suit and expensive shoes.

Cleo put down the unexpected heat rising up her neck to the clothes, not the man. She just wasn't used to power dressing.

He walked toward her, and she gulped again. "I was able to get out a day early," he said. "I wanted to see you."

Without thinking, Cleo rose from behind her desk. Her simple, Oxford-cloth cotton dress was probably wrinkled from a morning of sitting, and she automatically tried smoothing it with her palm. "You wanted to see *me?*"

He nodded.

Cleo tried slowing everything—her footsteps toward him, her pulse, her explanation that Jonah was with her mother. But then she stood in front of him and she wanted to touch his golden hair more than she wanted to kiss his mouth, and she wanted to kiss his mouth more than she wanted him to touch her.

Slow down, she reminded herself again. This is the man who gave you a piece of property as a thank-you gift.

With a renewed sense of self-preservation, she took a step back. "Why did you want to see me, Ethan?"

"Because, uh…" He blinked, as if the why hadn't occurred to him. His hand reached out and tucked a stray tendril of hair behind her ear.

Goose bumps prickled on her cheek and ran down the too-warm skin of her neck. No. She took another step back. Sure, she wanted him to want her, but she wanted to make certain he was moved by passion and desire, not by convenience and gratitude.

She cleared her throat. "Your trip was successful?"

He nodded, and his expression suddenly lightened. "I know what I came to tell you," he said, grinning. "I just, uh, forgot for a minute."

Despite the temptation of that gorgeous grin, Cleo retreated one more step, the backs of her thighs hitting the edge of her desk. She leaned against it, but couldn't help smiling a little in return. "Good news?"

"Great news." His grin widened.

Cleo folded her arms over her chest to stop herself from reaching out and tracing his mouth with her fingertips. "Okay," she said. "Out with it."

"The Covingtons have dropped their suit."

For a moment Cleo puzzled over the unfamiliar name. But then it hit her. "Jonah's grandparents?" She couldn't put a name to the euphoric bubble that burst inside her. "Jonah's grandparents have given up fighting for custody?"

Ethan's answering grin made her head spin. "Yep."

Cleo didn't know what was wrong with her. The edges of the room started going black and Ethan seemed too far away. "He's going to stay with you?" she said over the lump in her throat.

"He's going to stay with *us*."

The room shrank to a tunnel.

"Cleo? Cleo?" She heard Ethan's voice but, like the rest of him, it was distant. Then large warm hands grasped her shoulders. The funny thing was, she thought dazedly, she knew those were Ethan's hands, even though he was so very far away.

"Cleo, honey." He pulled her up against his chest. "Breathe, honey. Breathe."

As instructed, she sucked in a breath. Then another. The room lightened, the tunnel opened up and suddenly her vision completely cleared and she was staring at the lapel of an olive-colored, light-weight wool suit jacket.

Ethan took her chin in his hand and made her look up. His gaze ran over her face. "Your color's coming back. Are you all right? What was wrong?"

Cleo licked her lips. "I knew…I knew you were going to see your attorney in Houston about the custody, but I didn't let myself think about it."

He frowned, his eyebrows coming together over his concerned blue eyes. "Okay."

"And you'll notice I didn't ask you about it, even though we talked almost every night."

He nodded. "And I didn't say anything to you, because there wasn't anything to tell until today. I visited the Covingtons, too, and told them about you and about our marriage, but I wasn't sure of their response."

Cleo swallowed to ease her dry mouth, aware of what she'd been hiding from. *I was supposed to be the reason they would let you have Jonah*, she wanted to say. *I was terrified I wouldn't help.*

What would their marriage have been about then?

And she had been hiding from something else, too. She hadn't acknowledged how worried she'd been about one more thing. One more very important thing.

He frowned again. "What aren't you telling me, Cleo? I want to know why you almost fainted on me a minute ago."

She bit her bottom lip. "Oh, Ethan," she said. Tears stung the corners of her eyes and she blinked them back. "I don't think I could bear to lose him." The truth was wrenched from her heart. "I've been too scared to even think about it. I care about that little boy so much."

The tears in Cleo's eyes kept her from seeing Ethan's expression, but it didn't matter, because he jerked her against him and held her close. "Cleo." He murmured her name gruffly. "Oh, Cleo."

She wrapped her arms around his waist and breathed in Ethan's scent. His solid warmth comforted her. "Thank God, we get to keep Jonah."

His cheek rubbed against the top of her head. "Thank God," he echoed.

"I didn't know how easy it would be to love him," she said.

Ethan stilled. Two heartbeats passed, and then he pushed her a few inches away, just enough to look down into her face. "Cleo..." he said hoarsely.

She reached up and touched his mouth, just as she'd been wanting to. "What?" she whispered.

There was something in his eyes she'd never seen before. His fingers tightened on her shoulders. "I wish—"

"Am I interrupting something?" boomed a loud, male voice.

Cleo automatically swung toward the door, breaking her connection with Ethan. He stepped away, and she stared at the newcomer in her office. "Stuart?" she said stupidly, her mind still caught up in Ethan's embrace and the second time he'd started an "I wish" that he couldn't finish.

Her longtime friend Stuart Smith smiled wickedly and leaned one rangy shoulder against the doorjamb. "Forgotten me already?" His gaze flickered toward Ethan. "You won't be forgiven, sweetheart, unless you tell me that this guy in the Eye-talian apparel is your brand-new husband."

She ignored his "Eye-talia"—she'd punish him later by telling his Nona Marchetti, who would then withhold Stuart's favorite cannoli dessert—and made quick introductions. "This is my husband, Ethan Redford. Ethan, this comedian here is a half-Italian cowboy with the unlikely name of Stuart Smith."

Stuart shook Ethan's hand. "Ropin' and rigatoni. With one I caught Cleo. But it was the other that held her." His smile took on that wicked edge again. "Do you know how much Cleo loves pasta, Ethan? Well, any kind of food if a man is cooking for her. It's because—"

Cleo gripped Stuart's forearm and dug in her fingernails. "Are you looking for your daughter? Bessie is probably at storytime with the four-year-olds." She tugged him in the direction of her doorway. "Don't let us stop you."

Stuart winced, but the teasing light didn't leave his eyes as he firmly planted the heels of his cowboy boots into her carpet. "Something tells me Ethan doesn't know that you once wore my ring."

"I didn't know." A funny expression crossed Ethan's face and he looked at her. "You wore another man's ring?"

Stuart chuckled and Cleo shot him a mean look. He always did have lousy timing. When he saw that she and Ethan were…close, couldn't he have just left them alone?

She sighed. "I wore Stuart's *class* ring. I was fifteen years old."

The teasing was gone from the tall cowboy's brown eyes, leaving only fondness behind. "For two years, though, Cleo. You wore it for two years, and it was the darkest day of my life when you took it off and gave it back to me."

Her jaw dropped. "Stuart, you went out with Dinah Marcus behind my back. *Two times.*"

Stuart nodded. "I was an idiot." He looked over Cleo's head at Ethan. "Don't be stupid, Ethan," he said, and Cleo thought he even sounded a bit serious. "Don't let go of this woman."

There was an ironic edge to Ethan's voice. "I've heard that from more than one man, believe me."

Cleo shook her head. Men were so funny sometimes. "You big silly," she said to Stuart. She went on tiptoe to kiss his cheek, and then pat it, as if sealing it there. "Dinah Marcus went on to become your wife, and a happier couple I've never met. You don't have to pretend anything for Ethan. He sees me for what I am."

And then she frowned at the disquieting notion. Was she really just the practical, sensible woman he thought?

Stuart bent to give her a goodbye peck on the mouth. "I know *exactly* what Ethan sees, sweetie-pie." With a two-fingered salute and laughter in his eyes, he left them.

Cleo pursed her lips and turned toward Ethan, shaking her head. "That man…"

The strange, intense look on Ethan's face had her stumbling over her tongue. He walked toward her with purpose and she found herself stepping back, toward the safety of the open door.

Ethan continued to advance. "I've been wondering, Cleo." His words were thoughtful, though his voice was tight. "Have you dated and kissed and broken the heart of every man in Montana, or just Whitehorn?"

Cleo's eyes widened. Her hands found the knob of the door, and she hung on to its solidness. There was something new in the way Ethan was looking at her, something she'd barely remembered from months ago when they had first met. There was a kiss in his eyes. Suddenly nervous, she squeezed the knob.

He must have noticed. "What a good idea," he said. In one fluid movement, he plucked her fingers free and kicked the door shut with his foot.

Six

Driven by impulse, Ethan took hold of Cleo by her upper arms and maneuvered her back against the now closed door of the office. She licked her lips nervously and the coil inside him heated and tightened.

"Ethan?"

"Mmm." His muscles were tense, too, and he didn't know if it was because of the three airport terminals he'd sprinted through to make his Montana flight, or because of something else.

"Um, you know that Stuart was only teasing me… you…um, I guess us."

Oh, yeah, and it was just about as funny as he was feeling right now. Annoyed-as-hell funny. Because when he'd first walked into her office just the sight of her had wiped everything else from his mind. He'd wanted to taste her ripe mouth and put his hands on her ripe curves and take her, take her, take her.

But when he'd come to his senses and told her about the Covingtons's decision, she'd floored him again. Knocked him flat on his butt by the depth of her feelings for Jonah.

God. He'd never known a woman who cared this much. The tears in her eyes had been more precious than diamonds, and it had half thrilled and half chilled him that he realized it…and yet couldn't offer her anything as valuable in return.

Ethan Redford was a man who always paid his debts. But he suspected Cleo's bill was something he could never clear. He would never have that much cash.

Or whatever else she wanted it paid in.

"Ethan."

He ignored her, and the fact that his bill was just about to go up. Way up.

That hot coil was burning inside him with undeniable insistence. It had been twisted and heated by every man he'd watch kiss her, by every man who had known her longer than he had, by every man who had at one time wanted her.

She was his now.

And he was going to have her.

He lowered his head and brushed her lips with his. Sweet. Cleo tasted like a sugary treat.

He'd known from the beginning she'd be bad for him.

He stroked her mouth another time and she made a little sound, but he didn't even bother to figure out what it meant. He wanted more. The sweet taste of Cleo's mouth was just too good.

He crowded her against the door and kissed her again. Her lips were soft and pliant but he didn't even try to open them with his tongue. He wanted to, damn, he wanted it bad, but anticipation was almost as addictive. And he had to prove to himself he had some kind of control when it came to her.

She made another noise and wiggled against him. He groaned and his hands left her upper arms. To hold her head still, he drove his fingers into her hair, and then bent again to her soft lips.

Control, he reminded himself. Anticipation. He brushed against her lips, brushed once, twice, but when she made that anxious little noise again, he couldn't stop himself from following her breath inside her mouth.

Anticipation fled. Control disappeared. Inside Cleo's wet heat, Ethan lost all sense of timing, all notion of the tactics that made him a winner in the boardroom. He pressed his tongue deeper, pressed his heavily aroused body against her belly.

Her arms looped around his neck. She lifted herself against him, tilting her hips to move him closer. His heart ricocheting in his chest, he angled his head to explore her mouth from another direction, and he rubbed his tongue along hers.

Her body jerked against him, and the movement made him lift his head. Her mouth was wet and her violet eyes were at an erotic half-mast. He groaned silently, needing her again, more, closer.

Desperate to touch, he ran his palms down her back to cup her round bottom. He shuddered and instantly craved more.

"Cleo," he whispered. His mouth trailed over her lips, her cheek, and down her neck. He wanted to devour her, in huge gulping bites.

He rubbed his pelvis against hers and that coil of desire inside him wound tighter. His fingers moved with a will of their own, pulling up the fabric of her long dress in great bunches. As he took her mouth, thrusting his tongue inside, he thrust his hands beneath her silky panties.

Her silky skin filled his palms.

She moaned.

Something slammed hard in his chest, as if it was knocking against it.

The something slammed again, and the knocking—

Someone was knocking on Cleo's office door.

Ethan lifted his head, withdrew his hands, stepped back. Her skirt fell around her calves like a curtain going down on pleasure.

She stared at him.

He buttoned his suit jacket to hide his erection.

Cleo was still staring at him, despite another insistent knock.

"Cleo, someone's at the door," he said.

She blinked.

"And if it's another one of your old boyfriends," he said flatly, "I can promise you blood will be shed."

Blinking again, she whirled around and opened the door. Maybe it was because of his threat that Cleo stepped into the hall, leaving him alone with his thoughts…and his lust.

He dropped into an empty chair, rubbing his palm over his face. What the hell was he doing?

If he wanted to seduce Cleo—and God knows he did, but he still wasn't at all sure it was right—why had he acted like a oafish hothead and pushed her against the door and then pushed his tongue in her mouth?

The slow tease, the gradual courtship, and then the well-timed union of two separate entities were steps he'd studied in business school and then perfected in the business world. Wooing a woman had never been any different for him. Or to him.

But with Cleo… When it came to Cleo he forgot all his lessons and let impulses, neediness, and cravings drive him.

He hungered for her in a way that was at once familiar and terrifying. He'd experienced that single-minded focus at work before. It was a hunger that reminded him too much of the anger that had been his father's driving force.

An anger that led him to hit and rage…all in the name of love.

Ethan's gaze snagged on Jonah's portable crib, tucked away in the far corner of Cleo's office. A corduroy elephant stared at him down his long, long nose, and a yellow bunny sat up on its fluffy tail. Ethan sighed.

He wasn't afraid he'd ever physically hurt Cleo. God, he knew he could never raise his hand to her, or any woman or child.

But there were other ways to cause her pain. If they became intimate, she would have every right to demand from him the depth of caring that she herself was capable of. And Ethan just didn't have that to offer. He had a sick feeling that he had *nothing* to offer Cleo.

Because growing up with a man such as Jack Redford hadn't shown Ethan how to be a husband and father. Only how not to be one.

When Cleo walked into the house with Jonah that evening, she was met by the delicious smell of pizza. Relief mingled with the awkwardness of seeing Ethan again after this afternoon's mind-blowing kisses. She'd managed to avoid the whole cooking issue so far in their marriage. And today of all days, she didn't think she would have been able to pull off a meal even the least bit palatable.

Not when the only thing she could think of was the heady sensations of his hands in her hair and on her skin, of his mouth so soft one minute and so greedy the next.

She shivered as Ethan walked out of the kitchen. To smooth over the moment, she held up Jonah. "Here he is! My mother was sorry to have caused you to miss him." After their…interlude, Ethan had quickly left Beansprouts and told her he'd meet her at home.

Cleo approached Ethan and lifted Jonah toward him. Instead of taking the proffered baby, Ethan slipped the overstuffed diaper bag off her shoulder. "Let me get this," he said.

Her eyebrows rose, but she didn't say anything as Ethan set the bag on a nearby table. When he turned, she tried for a natural smile. "Pizza, huh? Shall I serve us while you entertain Jonah for a bit?"

Ethan's gaze shifted away from the baby. "Let me serve you," he said quickly.

Cleo narrowed her eyes. Ethan needed to spend time with Jonah and vice versa. If they were going to build a family, that is. And with the memory of those kisses as incentive, she was determined that they both give this marriage a real go.

Without giving him a chance to get away, she walked to Ethan and thrust the baby into his arms.

He automatically grabbed hold of him, thank goodness, though he appeared as if he didn't want to. Without a backward look, Cleo headed into the kitchen.

Ethan trailed behind. "What do I, uh, do, exactly, to entertain him?"

Cleo slid him a glance. He stared down at the baby as if Jonah were a piece of fruit Ethan couldn't quite figure out how to peel. She almost relented and took the baby from him, but then she remembered how happy he'd been to tell her that Jonah's grandparents were giving up their custody battle. Ethan wanted the little boy in his life, no doubt about that.

"Cleo?"

She ignored the tiny note of panic in his voice. "You can keep me company in the kitchen. Jonah will let you know if he finds it boring." At the sink, she washed her hands and then tied on an apron.

She slid another look at Ethan. He still held the baby stiffly, a couple of inches away from his body, as if he wanted some distance between them. Pursing her lips, she breathed out a silent, frustrated sigh.

Distance was the problem. Ethan's job allowed for plenty of physical distance between the three of them, and she'd known from the start that Ethan liked to keep an emotional distance, too.

She didn't know why.

When they'd met months ago he'd been the same. Then, he'd talk to her, the conversation easy and charming, but he'd share nothing of himself. Now, despite the fact they were married, he was as reticent. Even during their nightly phone calls, the subject matter had never been anything personal.

Cleo took silverware from the drawer and began setting the table. Ethan leaned against a nearby countertop, looking uncomfortable. She ached to tell him to hold Jonah against the warmth of his body. She ached to ask him to hold *her* against him again.

Never before had passion risen so hot and so fast inside her. If he'd asked, she'd have made love to him right there in her office! Well, maybe she was a little too sensible for that, but she'd have gone somewhere with him. Gone anyplace they could be alone and indulge in touching and kissing and—

Cleo had to shove her hands into the apron pockets so he wouldn't see them shaking. Only a fool wouldn't realize there could be something special between her and Ethan. But their marriage wouldn't go anywhere if she couldn't get him to open up to her.

She didn't want to be married to a stranger, no matter how passionate that marriage could be.

The pizza took only a moment to serve. When they sat at the table, with Jonah in his infant seat as a centerpiece, Cleo bit into her slice with relish.

"Nothing beats pizza," she said after swallowing the first mouthful.

Ethan cocked an eyebrow her way. "Pizza's number one with you? That surprises me."

"Why?"

He shrugged. At some point before she'd come home he'd changed from a suit to jeans and a T-shirt. Ethan without his Armani always took a little getting used to. "I would have thought you'd like something...I don't know, more sophisticated, maybe."

Cleo set her slice down on her plate. "Sophisticated? Me?"

He shrugged again. "You forget. I've eaten a lot of meals at the B and B. It's the kind of fare a person could get used to. You've been around that for quite some time."

"It's Jasmine who's in charge of the food. Not just the breakfasts for the guests. She's always experimenting. So most of what I've eaten has been Jasmine's choice and Jasmine's cooking." Someday Cleo was going to have to admit to Ethan that not only was delivery pizza the best dinner she could imagine, but the best dinner she herself knew how to prepare.

"Do you, uh, like sophisticated food best?" she asked. If he answered in the affirmative, she would definitely have to break the news that all that kind of cooking was going to have to be done by him.

"Mmm. I don't know."

Cleo frowned, tamping down a little spurt of irritation. See, even in the littlest things he wouldn't open up to her. If Mr. Armani had grown up on foie gras and imported truffles, what was the harm in telling her?

She picked up her pizza slice again and then looked him straight in the eye. "What's the best meal you've ever eaten?" she asked.

"Easy," he answered promptly. "October 1998. The Field House in St. Helena, California. It's a small restaurant in the wine country." He smiled. "I ate lunch there and then I offered to make them rich."

Cleo wondered if he'd shared that special lunch with a woman. "Rich, how?"

"I offered them the capital to open a place in New York or San Francisco." Ethan chuckled. "I begged them to do something in Houston so I could eat there more regularly. But they turned me down flat."

"They?" she asked.

"A husband and wife team. But the two of them liked St. Helena. They liked raising their children in a small town."

"Like Whitehorn," Cleo found herself saying.

Ethan lifted his water glass in a little toast. "Like Whitehorn."

Cleo gave her attention back to her pizza.

"How about you?" he said. "What's the best meal you ever had?"

Cleo pursed her lips, then lowered her voice to a whisper. "You have to promise never to tell my mother."

Ethan's mouth twitched. "Why?"

She shook her head. "Promise first."

He smiled now. "I promise."

Cleo leaned over her plate and whispered, "My cousin Summer, Jasmine and I had a party at the house once."

Amusement lit Ethan's eyes. "So?"

"I can't remember where the adults were—my mother, my aunt and uncle—but they thought we were old enough to stay overnight alone. We invited just a few girlfriends over, but…" She gave him a knowing look.

His eyebrows rose and he sat back in his chair. "I'm guessing you had a few more guests than you expected."

She nodded sagely. "And they were boys."

"Cleo," Ethan said, amusement in his voice, but his expression harder to read, "have you been a man magnet since the day you were born?"

"'Man magnet'?" She waved the idea away. "Yeah, right. When you are sandwiched between two beauties like Summer and Jasmine, you get real used to being the ordinary one."

"The 'ordinary one'?" Ethan echoed. "You've got to be kidding."

She appreciated how surprised he sounded, she

really did, but she was the practical, sensible, capable one, correct?

"Hey," she said. "I accepted it long ago and I don't mind, honest. I'm the girl that was every guy's buddy. You know, the one who'd introduce them to the girl they didn't have enough nerve to strike up a conversation with. The one they'd take to a dance because they didn't need to impress me. If a guy got in a jam, he knew he could turn to me for advice or…whatever."

Ethan's brows came together. "What's 'whatever'?"

"Maybe he needed the notes from biology class. Maybe an idea for the perfect gift for his girlfriend." She shot him a look. "Maybe he needed a wife."

Ethan straightened. "Cleo—"

"But anyway, back to my party and the best meal I've ever eaten. So about a zillion kids show up, and we don't know how to turn them away. Or maybe we didn't try *that* hard, I don't know. But we paid, believe me. We spent the entire night turning the stereo down and rescuing furniture from irreparable damage and shutting the refrigerator and kitchen cabinets after the latest forage.

"It was 2:00 a.m. before the last partygoer was gone and we'd finished filling four trash bags. Summer drove off to find a place to dump them so Mama wouldn't find out. Jasmine and I sat in the kitchen and ate the only food left in the house. I was so relieved and so hungry that it is indelibly etched on my brain as the best meal of my life."

Ethan looked amused again. "And it was…?"

"Cap'n Crunch cereal. Brownies that weren't fully cooked—we couldn't wait that long to eat them. And pizza. The kind that comes frozen in a box and isn't much more than a saltine cracker with tomato sauce and a sprinkle of cheese."

"That's disgusting." He pushed his plate away.

"Hey, don't knock it until you're that hungry and have been that terrified your friends are going to break a lamp or something."

"It's still disgusting." He gave her a mock frown. "And promise or no promise, I just might tell your mother on you. You girls could have gotten yourselves in a bad situation."

"Don't go holier than thou on me now." Cleo wagged a finger at him. "You can't tell me you didn't crash a few girls' parties in your time." She tried imagining him as a teenager. Blond, and with that devastating smile. No girls would have hesitated to welcome him in.

Ethan was quiet for a moment, his gaze distant. "I crashed a few parties, all right," he said slowly, as if he wasn't aware he was speaking. "The kind thrown by untouchable girls who loved the darkest corners and the daring idea of taking the dirt-poor boy from the wrong side of town into them."

"What?" Cleo tried putting it together. *Dirt poor.*

The boy from the wrong side of town. No. Not Ethan. Not the man who wore European suits the way other men wore baseball caps.

"I wouldn't have come to your party, though, Cleo."

She was still grappling with the first insight he'd ever given her into his past. Ethan hadn't grown up rich, as she'd always thought. He'd been poor, dirt poor. "You wouldn't have come to my party?" she echoed stupidly. "Why not?"

"Because I would have known you weren't ordinary. Not ordinary at all." He pushed away from the table. "And I wouldn't have wanted to taint that."

Cleo just stared at him, her jaw agape. "You're not— You're not—" What did she want to ask? He didn't think she was ordinary? He was afraid he might taint her? "You're not going anywhere, are you?" she finally finished lamely.

"Not until I apologize."

Again, she stared at him dumbly.

"Listen. I grew up with a rough, brutal man. I'd cut off my right arm before I was ever either one to you, Cleo." He looked away, out the window, where it was just beginning to go dark. "So I'm sorry for the way I…kissed you today. So very, very sorry."

Before she could say anything in return, he was gone.

Cleo might have sat there all night, stunned, if it hadn't been for Jonah. He began to fuss and she left the dishes where they were to fetch his bottle, feed him, and then get him ready for bed.

Once he was finally tucked into his crib and asleep, Cleo let herself think about Ethan again.

Dirt poor. Wrong side of town. Father was a rough and brutal man.

She didn't know Ethan Redford. She didn't know him at all.

She'd married a stranger. A stranger who might have very good reasons for the distance he liked to keep. And one who felt he needed to apologize for the most passionate, most exciting kisses of her life.

Cleo wanted her mother.

Once she drove to the B and B and located Celeste reading in the den off the kitchen, Cleo found herself tongue-tied. Maybe it was because of the love seat—where she'd first encountered the power of what Ethan could do to her. Maybe it was because she couldn't explain how someone as capable as herself was married to a man who ran from emotional entanglements.

But she had to say *something* about why she was there. So despite the fact that a phone call would have served the purpose, she smiled and said she'd come by to share some interesting news she'd heard at the day care center. One of the Beansprouts's fathers worked on a construction crew at the Laughing Horse casino and resort project.

Cleo settled beside Celeste on the cushions. "So, Mama. You'll never guess," she said lightly. "Whitehorn has another mystery."

"What kind of mystery?" Celeste turned her way. With the light of a nearby lamp falling on her mother's face, Cleo could see the signs of more sleepless nights. She hadn't noticed it earlier in the day, when her mother's delight in Jonah hid so much.

Cleo's stomach clenched with worry, but she gamely continued. "They halted construction on the resort today." She widened her eyes in mock alarm. "Because they found a skeleton."

"What?" Celeste's book slid off her knees and thumped to the floor. "Did you say a skeleton?"

Cleo nodded.

Her mother leaned over to pick up her book, her wavy hair hiding her face. "You mean, like an animal's, or a dinosaur or something?"

"Nope. A human skeleton. And what's more, they found a bullet lodged in one of the ribs."

Celeste didn't immediately straighten, though it still took Cleo a couple of seconds to realize her mother was frozen with…with what?

"Mama?" She put her arm around Celeste's back and eased her to a sitting position. *Thump.* The book Celeste had retrieved fell again, out of her fingers this time, and Cleo kicked it aside and edged closer to her mother. "Mama?" She reached for Celeste's hands.

They were icy. The kind of cold that comes with shock…or terror.

Cleo pulled at the afghan tossed over the arm of the love seat and wrapped it around her mother. "What's wrong? Are you ill?"

When her mother didn't answer, Cleo jumped up. "I'm calling nine-one-one."

"No!" Celeste suddenly came to life, her gaze jumping to Cleo's face. "I'm all right, sweetie." She inhaled a shuddering breath. "Just a…just a goose… walking over my grave."

But to Cleo, Celeste looked as though she was going to be sick. "Mama—"

Her mother held up a hand. Cleo thought it was trembling. "Some tea, sweetie. I'll be fine after some hot, sweet tea."

"Are you sure?" At her mother's nod, Cleo backed toward the kitchen. "Lucky for you, tea is the one thing I don't burn." She was relieved when her mother smiled, and then even added a rusty chuckle.

The teakettle couldn't sing fast enough. Cleo checked on her mother fourteen times before the scent of steeping cinnamon and orange tea filled the kitchen and she was able to bring in a tray with the pot, two mugs, and a plate of Jasmine's heavenly tasting thumbprint cookies.

After a few sips from her mug, and one of the cookies, Celeste did appear better. Her color was back to normal and her hands seemed perfectly steady.

Cleo cradled her own mug and decided it was time to get tough with her mother. First it was the nightmares, and now this. "Mama," she said, her voice brooking no nonsense. "Mama, you must tell me what's wrong."

But another sip of tea seemed to infuse Celeste with a backbone even steelier than Cleo's. She pinned her daughter with the sharpest of gazes. "Cleo, sweetie, it's past dinner. Your baby's asleep and your husband just returned from a long trip away. But instead of being at home with him, you're visiting your mother. 'Tell me what's wrong'? I think that's my line."

Seven

Cleo stared into her mug of tea. Even though she'd come to her mother hoping Celeste would show her a way through this mess, it wasn't easy to admit to making a mistake. Especially when her family had taken her decision to marry Ethan with such aplomb. They'd been surprised, sure, but their faith in her good sense and practicality had reassured them she was making the right decision.

Instead, good sense hadn't played into her decision at all. She'd followed her heart—a heart that had done something as silly as falling in love at first sight.

Cleo didn't even know how to describe it to her mother. But one evening last January she'd wandered through the living room, her gaze on the magazine in her hand. Completely by accident, she'd smacked into Ethan, *his* gaze apparently distracted by the magazine in *his* hand. *Bump*.

Their gazes had met.

Her heart had landed at his feet.

Still without looking at her mother, Cleo now ran one finger around the rim of her mug. "Mama, why did you marry Daddy?" Cleo could barely remember her father, Ty Monroe, who had died in a car accident when she was a young child. Her memory held nothing at all of her parents' relationship.

"Not for the best reasons," Celeste said quietly.

Cleo looked up, startled. "What do you mean?"

Celeste sighed and gave a little smile. "The past just doesn't want to leave me alone."

"Oh, Mama." Cleo put out her hand, not wanting to cause her mother any discomfort. "We don't need to talk about it."

Celeste smiled again. "Maybe we do. I think it's time to shed light into some very dark corners."

"Mama…" Cleo said doubtfully.

Celeste patted Cleo's hand. "I think you need to hear this as much as I need to say it."

Cleo still had her doubts. But she set her tea on the tray and relaxed against the cushions of the love seat. "I'm listening."

Celeste took a sip from her mug. "You know about my older brother Jeremiah, about the kind of self-ish, controlling man he was. After our father died, he took over the lives of us three sisters, of Blanche,

Yvette and me. I don't know if it was out of a sense of protectiveness or just because he liked manipulating people."

"But, Mama, why didn't you and Aunt Yvette and Aunt Blanche break free of him?"

Celeste shook her head. "It seems like we should have, doesn't it? And Yvette did. She moved to Bozeman to get her teaching degree. But those were different times for most women, sweetie. We were expected to live under Jeremiah's rule—and his thumb—until we married."

"You told me once that you received three marriage proposals when you were in your twenties. You weren't tempted to accept one of them to get away from Jeremiah?"

Celeste smiled sadly. "Perhaps I should have. But I was waiting for…magic, I suppose."

Magic. Cleo knew all about that. It was one accidental meeting and then one heart lost. "But you didn't find it with Daddy, either?"

"I wish I could say I did, sweetie." Celeste lifted a hand to run her palm over Cleo's hair. "But as I got older, Jeremiah's reins on me became tighter and tighter. On Blanche, too."

Celeste lapsed into silence, and Cleo saw her forehead pleat, as if she were trying to figure out a puzzle or trying to remember a particularly fuzzy memory. "Then," Celeste went on, her gaze distant, "Raven disappeared. You know, Raven Hunter, the man Blanche loved and your cousin Summer's father. After Raven was gone, living with my brother became unbearable for me. Jeremiah always telling me what to do, how I should think, what I should say."

"Oh, Mama." Cleo hated the distress in her mother's voice. She couldn't imagine being treated that way by family, not when hers had always been unfailingly supportive and loving.

Celeste ran another gentle hand over Cleo's hair. "You know, that time is all so murky for me. But I *do* remember Jeremiah introducing me to Ty—your father. He was charming and he made me feel pretty and special." She smiled. "Your father was a good man, Cleo. Never doubt that. I just think he deserved more than a wife who wanted to move away from her brother more than she wanted him."

Cleo sighed. "So you think a marriage can't work without that…magic you were talking about?" And what about one-sided magic? How far could that take a marriage?

"I think a marriage takes more than magic. It takes patience and compromise and understanding." Celeste chuckled. "But I'm sure the magic makes all that compromise a little easier to swallow."

Cleo thought back to her childhood. She remembered the shape of her father's face and his smile, and then she remembered him smiling at her mother.

"Daddy loved you, though, Mama. I'm certain of it."

Celeste nodded. "At first sight, he always said."

At first sight. Maybe it was a family trait. Or a family weakness. "But maybe one-sided magic is enough." Cleo spoke almost to herself.

"Well," Celeste answered, "I personally think that the magic takes two."

Cleo was unconvinced. Because what she felt was definitely magical, and Ethan fought feeling anything at all toward her.

She picked up her mug of tea, cold now, and sipped anyway. How could she have fallen in love at first sight with such a man?

A beautiful man.

A successful, hardworking man.

A man willing to sacrifice his own lifestyle and convenience for the good of his sister's orphaned son.

Maybe loving Ethan wasn't so irrational, after all. Would those first feelings of attraction have survived if he were something less? And, anyway...

Cleo looked over at her mother who regarded her with an almost pitying gaze. "You don't just stop loving someone, do you, Mama?" Some messes just couldn't be cleared away by wishing them gone. "Just because it's not convenient or it's too difficult, it just doesn't stop, does it?"

Celeste's fingers were warm against Cleo's cheek. "I don't think so, sweetie."

After realizing that she couldn't stop loving Ethan even if she wanted to, Cleo decided her best course was to live up to her reputation and be sensible and practical about her convenient marriage. But it took a toll on her to remain calm and cool around him, so she was almost grateful when a few days later he announced he had to take another trip. Though Cleo had left a napping Jonah with Ethan a couple of times and biked into town to work for a few hours, most of her days were filled with the unrelenting awkwardness between them.

The one good thing she'd managed was to dodge the terrible truth of her cooking prowess—er, lack thereof—by volunteering to taste test a bunch of recipes Jasmine was working on. Every night she and Ethan sat down to a shared silence made enjoyable only by the wonderful stuff she picked up from the B and B's kitchen every afternoon.

So her mouth was full of some sort of delicious pasta when he said he was leaving the next morning, and she merely nodded. It was a darn good show of practicality.

She was just as cool when she followed him to the front door the next day. Wearing another one of his great suits and gripping his briefcase and one of those carry-on bags that only a man would find large enough, he was inches of irresistible deal-maker. She couldn't stop herself from reaching out and brushing a nonexistent piece of lint from the right shoulder of his gray suit.

He abruptly halted, then turned around.

Caught off guard, Cleo walked right into him.

He dropped his briefcase and caught her around the waist, as if to steady her.

She wasn't going to fall. That had already happened, of course, months ago.

But instead of stepping away, Cleo looked up at Ethan. He still held her lightly, and there was a fluttering in her belly where their bodies met.

"Cleo," he started. "I wish—"

In his crib down the hall, Jonah began fussing. Cleo turned her head, then looked back at Ethan. "Nap time's over early."

"He can wait a minute." Ethan tightened his hold on her waist. "I want you to know—"

The baby's fussing turned to crying.

Cleo tried ignoring the sound, but then broke from Ethan's embrace. "I'm sorry," she said, stepping away. She called softly down the hall, "Hang in there, buddy. Mommy's coming."

And at that one word—at "mommy"—the air became thick.

Mommy.

As if in slow motion, Cleo turned her head to see what Ethan made of her instinctive word. Maybe he hadn't heard it. Maybe he would resent her assumption.

Or maybe he would burn her with the bright, blazing blue that was in his eyes.

The rest of him had gone to stone, everything except for the hot intensity of his gaze. She felt the heat on her face, on her body. It wrapped around her like a binding.

"Thank you," he said hoarsely.

The words released her from the strange spell. She hurried down the hall, not even aware that Jonah was no longer crying until she entered his darkened room to discover he'd gone back to sleep.

Maybe she should stay in the baby's room until Ethan left. But that was cowardly. Worse, it would deny her one last glimpse of Ethan, and she was too weak to deny herself that, no matter how calm and cool she struggled to be.

And she wanted to gauge again what he thought of her calling herself Jonah's mommy.

He was still standing in the small foyer, exactly as she had left him. When she reappeared, he bent to pick up his briefcase. "Everything okay?" he asked.

She nodded. "He drifted off again."

The heat was gone from Ethan's eyes. "I know you'll take good care of him."

"Of course I will."

"Goodbye, Cleo."

She smiled, and then he turned and stepped

toward the door. With her feet rooted to the floor, she watched him turn the knob, and then he dropped his briefcase again and slid that improbably small carry-on off his shoulder.

The movements surprised her into retreating a step, but it didn't matter, because in milliseconds he caught up with her. "Cleo," he said, fisting his hand in the hair at the back of her head. He pulled gently, tilting up her face. "I don't want to leave you. Not without this."

And then he kissed her.

His mouth came down on hers, no softness in it whatsoever, and she opened up to him because there was nothing else but to give in to the demand of Ethan's tongue.

He filled her, hot and strong, and she leaned into his body, trying to get closer, closer, closer.

His groan was low and needy and she felt it purr against her breastbone. Cleo closed her eyes, thinking only of his indescribable taste when a shiver skittered over her spine and unmistakable passion rose again.

Only Ethan made her burn. Only Ethan could cause this sweet neediness to bubble inside her blood.

His mouth lifted off hers and she moaned, but he ignored her complaint, and pulled her head back farther so that he could kiss her neck. She felt the wet brush of his tongue below her ear and shuddered.

"Ethan," she whispered.

He came back to her mouth, biting gently at her lower lip. "I've got to get going," he said around another deep kiss.

She leaned harder against him and curled her arms around his neck. "No."

He groaned again, another purr against her breasts. "I need to make my plane."

"No," she said again.

He kissed her nose, then pulled back just enough to see her face. "If I get out of here now, it will be better for both of us."

Cleo stubbornly shook her head. "No."

"That's what you should be saying to *me,* Cleo. To what I want."

"No." She tightened her arms around his neck.

He groaned again, his expression half frustrated, half amused. "Cleo, I really, really have to leave. I hate it, I swear to God I do, but I don't have any choice."

He was right, of course. Meetings had been scheduled, appointments set. After one more delicious moment pressed against his body, she dropped her arms and sighed.

"All right." Despite how mad it made her, she felt tears sting the corners of her eyes.

To hide them, she looked down at her long skirt, as if inspecting for wrinkles. Cool and collected, right? That was what she'd promised herself to be. "Never say that I'm not sensible."

Two fingers caught her chin, tilted it up. "Oh, Cleo," he said quietly. "I could say that, and so, so much more."

With that surprising remark and one last kiss, he was gone.

But the surprises didn't end there. Before five o'clock that afternoon, a deliveryman shocked the heck out of her. Ethan had sent her another gift.

But nothing practical this time. The present was from one of her favorite shops in Bozeman. Inside a ridiculously tiny box was a heartbreakingly lovely crystal unicorn. She'd never seen anything like it. No bigger than a charm, it was strung on a delicate gold box chain.

The accompanying card wasn't in Ethan's hand-writing—obviously he'd ordered it over the phone and paid a mint to have it delivered the same day—but Cleo held it against her heart anyway. Because the only thing the card said was "You."

And though she didn't believe for a minute that Ethan considered her as rare and beautiful, as deli-cate and light-catching as the crystal unicorn, a sen-sible, practical woman such as Cleo Monroe—Cleo *Redford*—appreciated the thought.

Cleo wore the unicorn every day. Later that week, she was sitting at her desk at Beansprouts, absently fingering the crystal charm when a commotion in the reception area of the day care center caught her attention. Alarmed, Cleo first scooped Jonah up from his crib in the corner of her office and then stuck her head out her door.

A gaggle of strangers was insisting on speaking with her, while a just-as-insistent Nancy refused to open the waist-high swinging gate that led into the center.

Cleo put all her toddler-management skills into her voice. "What's the problem?" she called coolly as she approached Nancy.

Before the other woman could answer, she handed Jonah to her friend and asked her to take him into the break room. Then Cleo turned to the impatient group, placing her hand firmly on the swinging gate. "I'm Cleo Kincaid Monroe. Cleo Redford. What can I do for you?"

A blonde with a helmet hairdo and a sapphire suit stepped forward. "Elaine Eaton of KMNT, Ms. Monroe. Would you mind if I brought a camera crew inside?"

Cleo blinked. "I'd mind very much. There are small children here and I don't want them to be disturbed. What's this all about?"

Another reporter stepped up, aggressive and unsmiling. "You did say Cleo *Kincaid* Monroe?" he asked. "Niece of Jeremiah and Yvette Kincaid? Daughter of Celeste?"

Icy apprehension crawled down Cleo's back. On the desk nearby, a phone started ringing. "Celeste is my mother," she said. "Has something happened? Is she hurt?"

"What do you know about the skeleton?" asked the man.

"What?" Cleo said. Another line began ringing, and the phone's flashing lights jangled like her nerves. Skeleton? "What has happened to my mother?"

The man ignored her again. "We're looking for a comment from a Kincaid family member."

Forcing herself to stay calm, Cleo moved over to the desk and picked up the receiver. Ignoring the ringing, she punched a free line and speed-dialed the bed-and-breakfast. Busy signal.

The back of her neck as hot as the chill running down her spine was cold, Cleo turned to the group of strangers. *"Is there something wrong with my mother?"*

"As far as we know, your mother's fine," Helmet Head said, looking marginally sympathetic. "We want to know what Jeremiah Kincaid's family has to say about the skeleton."

"The skeleton?" The skeleton. The apprehension suddenly lifted and Cleo let out a shaky laugh. "This must be some mistake. You're talking about the Laughing Horse skeleton? We don't know anything."

Helmet Head lifted perfectly arched brows. "Are you sure about that?"

Cleo refused to let herself be scared again. "Of course. Now, I need to ask you people to leave—"

The aggressive man had pulled out a small note-book. "That's what you want us to print? That you don't know anything? Do you speak for your aunt and mother, too?"

Cleo stared. "I don't want you to print anything. I don't even know why you're asking me these questions. Now, if you won't leave my property, I'm going to have to—"

"Call the sheriff?" A new voice came from behind the small crowd of reporters. "I can save you the trouble, Cleo."

Over the heads of the strangers, Cleo spied the tall, dark figure of Sheriff Rafe Rawlings, the sharp creases of his uniform and the set of his face stating he was all business. She could kiss him. "I'm having a little problem, Rafe," she called. "Maybe you could help."

With his usual commanding, unsmiling demeanor, Rafe merely half turned to hold open the Bean-sprouts's front door. "Ladies, gentlemen, Ms. Monroe has asked you to leave." When they scurried toward him instead of immediately departing, he held up his free hand. "And I'm only here to pick up my daughter, not to answer any questions." One more pointed look, and the group moved outside, muttering.

Rafe quickly pulled the door shut.

Breathing a sigh of relief, Cleo perched on the edge of the reception desk, then looked at her watch. "It's a little early for you to pick up Skye from the arts and crafts program. Did someone call you?"

He nodded. "Nancy, and then Jasmine."

Cleo closed her eyes. "What's going on, Rafe?"

He grimaced. "Maybe we should go somewhere private."

Apprehensive once more, Cleo unlocked the swinging gate and led the way to her office. Once inside, Rafe shut the door and they sat beside each other on the chairs in front of her desk.

Cleo swallowed. "Why were the reporters here, Rafe? How does that skeleton found on the Laughing Horse property have anything to do with us?"

"It was actually found on *Kincaid* property, Cleo," Rafe corrected. He quickly reminded her that the construction had been halted on the resort, not the casino, when the skeleton had been discovered during excavation a couple of weeks before.

Rafe gave the next details in a matter-of-fact voice. "It took a little time, but we finally tracked down some dental records. The bones belong to Raven Hunter."

Raven Hunter. The name echoed in Cleo's mind and her stomach clenched into a tight fist. "Mama's going to be very upset," she said. And her mother already *was* upset, with those nightmares continuing to plague her. "Summer, too."

She looked up at Rafe, not sure how much Kincaid family history he knew. *Raven Hunter.* "Raven Hunter was the lover of my mother's sister, Blanche. He fathered my cousin, Summer."

Rafe nodded. "And disappeared during Blanche's pregnancy, right?"

Cleo rubbed her forehead. "That's the way I always heard it. The story was that Raven ran out on Blanche after getting her pregnant, maybe paid off by my uncle, Jeremiah Kincaid, maybe just because he didn't want to be tied down."

"No one in your family ever saw him again?"

"Not that I know of." Cleo looked up at Rafe again. "What does this mean?"

"There's the bullet, Cleo," he said.

Her stomach clenched again. Right. The skeleton had been found with a bullet lodged in one rib. Someone had killed Raven Hunter. Someone had killed Aunt Blanche's lover, Summer's father.

Cleo swallowed. "You're sure, Rafe? You're sure the bullet was the likely cause of death?" She knew his answer, even as she asked the question.

Rafe nodded.

Cleo swallowed again. "And the likely suspect is…?"

Rafe rubbed the back of his finger along his

jaw. "Your now-deceased uncle, Cleo. Jeremiah Kincaid."

Her eyes widened, and her temperature seemed to drop ten degrees. Not any of the family had ever really liked the man, but to think that he'd actually *murdered* someone...

She was still trying to wrap her mind around the idea when Rafe told her he had to leave. They stood and walked toward her closed office door. Before he could get away, Cleo rose on tiptoe to kiss his cheek. "Thanks for coming," she said. "I needed a hero."

Letting free one of his rare smiles, Rafe lightly hugged her with one arm. "My pleasure."

"I think I might have something to say about that."

Cleo whipped around. Ethan stood in the doorway of her office. She hadn't heard the door open.

Maybe Rafe had, because he was out-and-out grinning now. "This has to be the husband."

Ethan stepped forward. "I am. And you?"

Apparently he wasn't much impressed by uniforms, Cleo thought. She nudged him with her elbow. "For goodness' sake. How have you missed the big shiny badge? This is the sheriff, Ethan. Rafe Rawlings."

Rafe stuck out his hand and managed to swallow his huge grin. "And a *good* friend of Cleo's."

"Never doubted it," Ethan said, though when he

shook the other man's hand it was brief. "I'm sure you want to tell me all about it."

Rafe's lips twitched.

Cleo shot her husband a sharp look. "I thought you weren't coming home until tomorrow."

Ethan dragged a possessive thumb across her mouth. "Is that why I caught you kissing someone else? You didn't expect to see me?"

Rafe was smirking at them, so Cleo decided against answering the question. That, and she was fairly preoccupied fighting the hot tremor running across her skin.

It was Rafe who spoke into the strangely charged silence. "Actually, Mr. Redford, there was some trouble—"

"Here at Beansprouts that I needed Rafe's advice on." Cleo couldn't say what made her interrupt the sheriff, but suddenly she didn't want to bare this mess for Ethan right now. She could handle it herself. "Rafe's daughter Skye attends our summer arts and crafts program."

Rafe shot her a puzzled look, but took the hint and then just as smoothly took his leave.

Ethan folded his arms across his chest and narrowed his eyes. "What's the matter, Cleo?"

She avoided his gaze by bustling over to her desk. "I'm just…tired."

"Why don't we go home, then? It's almost five."

And she usually stayed past six. But Cleo looked

down at the paperwork stacked on her desk and then she looked up at the intense blue of Ethan's eyes. A little shiver tracked down her spine. She didn't know if it was because of what Rafe had told her, or because Ethan was back.

Suddenly she wanted to be home. Home with him.

"Okay," she said slowly. "Why don't you go ahead? I'll collect Jonah and be right behind you."

After Ethan left, Cleo made a quick call to Jasmine and discovered that the reporters had been at the B and B, too. But she'd gotten rid of them and Celeste seemed fine. Their mother was planning to have dinner and watch a movie over at Aunt Yvette's and Uncle Edward's house.

When Cleo arrived home from Beansprouts, Ethan was in his room unpacking. Rather than disturb him, Cleo decided to focus on Jonah for a few minutes to avoid thinking about the skeleton and how it was connected with her family.

The last of the sun made a bright patch on the living room floor, and Cleo spread a baby quilt in its warmth. Then she put Jonah down and lay beside him, his delight in her attention and her renditions of patty-cake and This Little Piggy taking some of the chilliness out of her mood.

But then, another set of shivers skittered down her back. Cleo looked up to see Ethan watching her and the baby, and something in his eyes made her shiver again.

"You're cold," he said.

Cleo stared at his mouth, suddenly remembering the last time they'd been together in the house, suddenly remembering their last, heated kiss. Another shiver. "A little cold," she said, and it was a little white lie to gloss over the real reason for her goose bumps.

He came closer and Cleo scrambled to her feet, nervous, silly enough, to be caught lying down around him.

Ethan's jeans were faded and he wore a white T-shirt that looked soft and comfortable. "Go take a hot shower," he said. "I'll take over with Jonah."

Cleo hesitated. Not that she wasn't happy that he was going to spend some time with the baby—he needed to do that—but because despite his casual words, there was that something in his eyes. Something that made her want to run and to linger at the same time.

"Cleo?" His gaze shifted from her eyes to her mouth.

Running seemed like a really good idea. "Uh, well, thanks." She backed out in the direction of her room. "There's a bottle of formula in the fridge."

He waved his hand. "I'll take care of it." His voice hoarsened. "You go get…warm."

Naked. She thought for a second he was going to say naked.

So this time she really ran.

Though she'd taken the longest shower on record, she still felt tense when she emerged. Even more tense when she heard the doorbell ring. She jumped. Please, no more reporters.

Determined to squash the problem immediately if it was, Cleo headed down the hall in bare feet and her own jeans and T-shirt, only to find that Ethan had beat her to the door and was paying off the pizza delivery kid.

He turned around, the box in his hands. "Jonah drifted off. I put him in his crib and ordered your favorite."

Cleo tried smiling through her relief. "Oh, good."

Ethan narrowed his eyes at her again. "What's wrong, Cleo?"

"I…" She didn't want to tell him about what happened that day. Exactly why, she wasn't sure. Maybe because he was home for once and she didn't want the evening marred by talk of a thirty-year-old murder. "I'm just a little unsettled."

At her answer, he gave her another narrow-eyed look, but let it go.

In the kitchen, they polished off the pizza without much conversation. She was preoccupied keeping her thoughts free of skeletons and bullets. She had no idea what was keeping Ethan so quiet.

When they finished, they both rose to clear away the few dishes. He set the pizza box on the counter and she loaded the plates in the dishwasher.

Her gaze snagged on the kitchen windows. It was dark and for the first time the giant shapes of the pines trees surrounding their house seemed menacing. Unbidden, all that she'd learned that day rushed to the forefront of her mind. Her uncle Jeremiah had been a murderer.

Nursery rhymes and hot showers couldn't wash that knowledge away. Her whole body shuddered.

"Cleo?" Ethan put a hand on her shoulder. "Are you okay, honey?"

She swallowed. "Just…cold again."

He stepped closer and wrapped his arms around her waist, pressing his chest against her back. He was big and warm, yet even the feel of him against her couldn't dispel her disquiet.

"Talk to me, Cleo."

Ethan tightened his arms, coaxing her to lean back.

She let herself sink against him and felt his breath stir the hair at her temples. She should talk to him, she should tell him what had happened today. A murder had been uncovered and it was connected to her family. But her blood was starting to warm. If she talked about it, she might turn cold again.

Ethan's arms tightened around her. "Cleo?"

She sighed. "Have you ever felt a nightmare coming on? Like a headache? Because that's just what I'm feeling."

Ethan stilled. "That's because you've been alone too much," he said.

She leaned farther into his warmth. "You think so?"

Suddenly his hot mouth was on the side of her neck. "You don't have to have nightmares, Cleo," he said against her skin. "Let me be there for you, honey. Let me make your dreams sweet tonight."

Eight

Ethan lifted his mouth from Cleo's skin and breathed in the sweet scent of her hair. He wanted to protect her. He'd vowed he would protect her.

If he couldn't offer emotion, he could at least offer that.

She laughed a little shakily. "I don't know…"

Ethan squeezed his eyes shut, trying to put out of his mind the sensation of her skin beneath his lips. "I'll just hold you, Cleo. That's all." He wanted it all, but he'd settle for watching over her sleep. It was time he gave something back.

"Oh."

A note in her voice—a touch of embarrassment?—made him open his eyes and turn her in his arms so he could search her face. "'Oh'? What does that mean?"

She looked down, her long lashes casting shadows on her flushed cheeks. "It means you don't have to go that far, Ethan. You don't need to…to share my bed."

A realization clicked in place in Ethan's brain. He stared down at Cleo—at his wife—stunned, trying to imagine how he'd made such a bad mistake. He let go of her, so mad at himself that he needed to pace around the room to ease the emotion. "Damn it, Cleo." One more turn around the too small kitchen, and then he stood in front of her again.

"Damn it."

She cocked an eyebrow, her expression wary. "I heard you the first time."

"And I think I screwed up *every* time," he said in disgust. "You didn't think— You must have realized— *Hell.*" He ran a hand through his hair. "Honey. Cleo."

She swallowed. "What?"

He cupped her shoulders with his hands. "You've got to know I want you."

She shrugged, her shoulders pushing against his palms. "As a caretaker for your nephew."

His hands tightened on her. "No, Cleo. As a woman in my bed."

Her violet eyes widened. He stared into them, thinking there wasn't another color in the world the color of Cleo's eyes. How could she doubt she turned him on? What kind of man gave a woman these kinds of doubts?

A man struggling to not hurt said woman. But Ethan shrugged the little voice away and pulled Cleo against him. He whispered against her ear, feeling a shiver run through her body. "I want you, Cleo. You've got to believe that."

As if she couldn't help herself, her hips arched against his. She laughed, shakily again. "Maybe I believe that."

He caught her hips, pressing her lightly against his hard erection. "Unmistakable evidence."

"Then why—"

"Because you've given so much already." He leaned forward to kiss her forehead. "I shouldn't ask for anything else."

"Ethan…" There was a touch of humor in Cleo's voice and a smile tugged at her lips. "Something tells me you know how to give back."

There was a touch of sultriness in her voice, as well, and he smiled. "I want to."

"I want, too," she said.

And it was that honesty that did him in. Ethan could handle "I want." He could meet it, match it, satisfy it. He ran his hands up her back to cup her face, holding it at the perfect angle for a gentle, deep kiss. She tasted warm and sweet and he wanted deeper and hotter, but he admonished himself to pull back. Go slow.

When he broke away, he combed his fingers through her bewitching, wavy hair, and his fingertips snagged on a chain around her neck. Tugging gently, from beneath her shirt he pulled the unicorn he'd given her. It caught the light and sparkled, shining like Cleo's eyes.

A smile broke over his face. "You like it." He wanted to see her wearing the unicorn and nothing else.

She shivered, maybe reading the intent on his face. "I like it."

I'm going to treat her like the unicorn. As she should be treated, Ethan promised himself. Precious and fragile. He would control his impulses tonight. Unlike his father, he wouldn't let his passions overrule him. Instead, Ethan vowed to use what had always stood by him—his brains—to make Cleo happy.

He let the unicorn drop and watched it fall to rest between her breasts. His gaze lifted slowly to her face. She was flushed more deeply now, and Ethan cupped her hot cheek gently. "Tell me where you want to make love," he said quietly.

Her pupils dilated.

"Tell me where you want me to touch you first."

"Ethan—"

"Tell me where you want me to touch you second, and third."

Her skin heated beneath his hand and her tongue came out to quickly wet her lips. "Ethan."

Her mouth was ripe and wet. A heat entirely his own shot down his spine, but Ethan ignored it. This was for Cleo. He rubbed his thumb along her cheekbone. "Embarrassed, honey?"

She ducked her head.

He ran his hands down her arms and then up beneath her breasts, to cup their weight in his palms. He ducked his head, too, so he could whisper against her ear again. "Why don't I tell you my ideas, and you can stop me if there's something you don't like or want to change."

"Ethan."

He lightly brushed his thumbs across her nipples and she shuddered. "I want to take you to my big bed. I want to undress you slowly. Piece by piece… Okay so far?"

Her lashes lifted but her gaze was languid. "Okay so far," she whispered. "But, Ethan—"

"Then I'm going to touch this pretty body of yours. Touch it, learn it, know it. Slowly."

She swayed closer. "But, Ethan—"

"Shh." He slid his hands from her breasts to cup her round bottom. "And once I know your body, honey, I'm going to please it. I'm going to please *you*."

Her hips arched, and he had to grit his teeth, willing himself to not push back. This was the time to go slow, to stay in control for Cleo. "Sound all right?" he asked.

"Ethan…" There was only an edge of purple around the black pupils of her eyes.

He clamped down on his impulses again, though his fingers tightened on the round curves they held. "You haven't told me what you think."

"I think—" Cleo reached up and tangled her fingers in his hair "—you talk too much."

His laugh died abruptly with the first electric touch of her mouth. His hold on her tightened again and she pressed herself closer in response.

Sensing she needed more, he deepened the kiss, but she sent him reeling by sliding her tongue into his mouth and against his.

His muscles tensed and his blood burned. He pulled her tighter against him, rocking her against his erection. She slid her tongue in deeper and he sucked, tasting sweetness and heat, and his mind emptied of everything but Cleo. He needed to feel her, see her, have her.

Without breaking the kiss, he let her slide back to the floor. His hands shook as he snaked them beneath the T-shirt she wore. Her skin was smooth and hot. He quickly found her bra strap and unhooked it so he could run his palms unhindered up her spine and around her ribs and then up her sides to fill his hands—*aaah*—with her breasts.

She jerked her mouth from his, gasping for breath,

and he closed his eyes, inhaling desperately. Cleo felt so good in his hands, heavy and full. Without thinking, he pulled off the annoyance of her shirt and slid the bra to the floor with one hand.

He could look his fill then, his heart slamming against his chest wall as her rosy nipples tightened.

"Ethan…"

Her hands rose, but he caught them before she could cover herself. Lacing his fingers with hers, he pushed her hands down, and then bent his head to one breast.

She smelled like flowers and tasted like sin.

She moaned, and he licked one beaded crest again, but the taste was too good, too tempting, and he sucked the nipple into his mouth.

She moaned again and the sound went to his head, making him dizzy. Somewhere along the way he dropped her hands, but it didn't matter, because she was holding his head to her body and letting him have his fill of her. He sucked at the other breast now, swirling his tongue around her nipple.

Her fingers crawled up his bare chest, beneath his shirt, inflaming him. He pushed her breasts together with his palms, wanting them both at once, wanting it all. Her nails scratched the skin of his back and he ran his tongue up her neck.

Her pulse was frantic, as needy as he felt. He took her mouth at the same moment that his hands met at the snap of her jeans. Goose bumps fanned out across her belly as he slid the denim down her body. He lifted her, and set her on the countertop wearing only a pair of silky white panties.

She grabbed at the hem of his T-shirt and he stripped it away, throwing it across the room. Then he stepped forward, pushing apart her thighs with his hips, so he could rub his chest against her damp, hard nipples.

He groaned.

She captured his head, bringing it to her for another kiss, and he met her mouth hungrily.

But the kiss, the sensation of breast to chest, still wasn't enough. There was fire inside him, fire inside her, and he wanted to touch it. Had to have it. Had to make it his.

The skin on the inside of her thighs was impossibly smooth. His fingers skimmed up it quickly, drawn toward the center of her. He reached the edge of her panties and lifted his head to gulp in a breath.

Only to see what he had done.

Impulsively, he'd bared her. In the kitchen. He had her on the counter, he had her open to him.

For his pleasure.

To satisfy him.

He'd been out of control.

Closing his eyes against the temptation of her lushness, he took in a long breath and softened his touch. "Cleo," he whispered. "Let me take you to the bedroom." Then he lifted her into his arms.

She looped her hands around his neck. He tried not to think of her breast against his chest or her breath against his ear. It soughed in and out, in a fast rhythm that almost matched the speed of his pulse.

He tried forgetting how close he'd been to sinking his fingers into her heated center, as uncontrollable as a teenager.

Now he thought only of Cleo.

His bedspread was cool against the backs of his hands as he slid her onto the mattress. He followed her down, but kept carefully to her side, thinking, *control, control, control.*

It was dark in his bedroom, and he set about learning her body all over again, this time listening for what made her breath catch. This time sensing what touch ignited goose bumps over her skin.

She moaned when he thrust his tongue in her mouth. She arched up to him when he took her nipple in his mouth. Her hands were restless along his back as he traced the delicate framework of her collarbone with his tongue.

All the while Ethan breathed Cleo in, her scent, her taste, and he fought against his darker instinct to push, to press, to possess. Tension infused her body, and his pulse quickened as she became bow-tight. But still he played and dawdled and felt damn good about his restraint.

"Ethan." Cleo's voice was breathy and she caught his hand against her breast as he played with her pretty nipple. "I—"

"Shh." He took her hand away and kissed her breast, letting his fingers trail down her abdomen. She jerked as he slid his hand beneath the elastic of her panties. He pressed his palm flat, letting her get used to this new sensation, and when she'd calmed he moved his fingers lower.

Her thighs opened wider for him, and as he slid a finger inside he lifted his head to watch her.

Her eyes closed as he found her wet heat, and then his did, too, because her body gripped him strongly, hotly. He fought the passion then, fought the need to have it, her, right that instant.

When control was back he allowed his hand to move again, sending Cleo higher. He took her to the edge—he saw it in her face, in the trembling he could feel in her muscles—and then he took his hand away.

"Please, Ethan." She reached toward him, caught her finger on a belt loop of his jeans. "Please."

"Yes, sweetheart." He shucked the rest of his clothes and rose over her, naked. "Now."

She parted her legs and he couldn't look, afraid he'd lose it. This was for her. For Cleo, first and foremost.

Hot, tight, wet. She sheathed him so completely that for a moment his mind spun. But he leashed his impulses and pulled out and slid slowly back in. She made a sound, sweet and low, and he went back to her breast to build a matching rhythm, slow and sure.

That tension built inside Cleo again, each of her breaths a little shallower than the one before. But the tension was in him, too, and with each thrust into her body he found control that much harder to keep.

"Please, Ethan."

He tilted her hips with his hands, drove deeper into her snug body, and she arched again. He kissed her, and she thrust her tongue deep.

He held control only by his fingernails. But he held on, because they were…almost…there. Cleo arched again, he angled his head deeper, and then the spasms shook her.

And him. It was a chain reaction of pleasure. They were climaxing, and it no longer mattered who controlled whom and who did what first and who drove whom to what.

Once he could breath again, Ethan eased off of Cleo and gathered her into his arms. The hollow of his shoulder cradled her cheek. He smiled.

What mattered was, at last, they'd found a way to ease the tension that had been building since the day they married. For once, he and Cleo had found an understanding.

Or so he thought. Because suddenly, into the

room heated with their passion, the sound of Cleo's three little words rushed out. "I love you."

Cleo stared at the luminous hands of the alarm clock beside Ethan's bed. It didn't seem as if there would be nightmares or sweet dreams for her tonight.

Not when her mind was occupied with running over every second of their lovemaking.

Ethan was spooned behind her, his hand heavy on her breast. She closed her eyes, savoring the sensation, aware of every inch where he touched her: hand, chest, his thighs against the backs of hers.

A sweet shiver ran across her skin and her nipple tightened against the cup of Ethan's palm. His breath moved rhythmically against her hair, so she could safely lust without his knowing about it.

Without making the mistake of saying she loved him again.

Her eyes popped open and she stared at the clock once more. Approximately sixty-seven minutes ago she'd uttered the words, and then immediately, desperately, wanted to grab them back.

What had possessed her to say them? It was all his fault. In the first place, there was the tremendous relief of knowing Ethan was truly sexually attracted to her. But then he'd overwhelmed her by the way he touched her, stroked her, stoked the fire of her passion for him. When her climax had nearly shaken her heart free of its moorings, the words had drifted from her heart to her mind and then out her mouth.

She couldn't be sorry they were finally in the same bed. Not only because of how good it was between them, but how good it was going to be for their marriage. Sharing a bed signaled a new intimacy that would definitely help in the building of a family.

But then again, there were still those words she'd said. The words he hadn't responded to, of course. Would a return to her own bed counterbalance them?

Too much emotion made Ethan nervous. Cleo was certain of that.

She straightened one leg and slid it across the cool expanse of sheet toward the edge of the mattress. Digging in her heel, she inched away from the heat of Ethan's body, trying not to moan as the movement dragged his palm over her bare breast.

Just as she scooted free, his arm roped her and pulled her back against his body. "Where do you think you're going?" His voice was hoarse and his breath hot against her ear.

Cleo was helpless against the shiver that rolled down her spine. "I—"

He turned her and covered her mouth with his. Cleo lost her words, her thoughts, her determination to leave his bed.

He thrust into her mouth with his tongue. His

hand pulled her thigh on top of his, and he thrust into her body, already wet and soft for him. Cleo gasped, arched against his chest, and another shudder rolled down her back.

Ethan chased it with his hands, and palmed her hips to tilt her body for another delicious thrust.

Cleo moaned, then silenced herself by pressing her face against his neck. She couldn't lose this. She couldn't lose him.

Cleo arched again as she took another thrust. She wouldn't leave his bed. She would hold on to Ethan...even if it meant holding back how she truly felt about him.

Nine

Cleo walked toward the back door of the B and B with Jonah, her mood as bright as the morning sunshine. She and the baby had woken at their usual early hour, but Ethan had slept on, either exhausted by yesterday's jet lag or by last night's lovemaking.

Her eyes narrowed as she hitched Jonah higher against her chest. Did he look a little flushed? She put her cheek against his, and he turned his head toward her, giving her what she could have sworn was a kiss. She smiled at him and he smiled back. "You angel." With a nose-to-nose nuzzle, she dismissed her little worry.

Nothing could take the sunshine out of today.

"Let's go find Auntie Jasmine," she said to Jonah. "You smile to distract her while I snitch some pastries." And if her mother insisted, Cleo thought, she'd leave Jonah with her for the morning and bring Ethan his breakfast in bed.

And if he wanted to feast on her—well, she hadn't had her fill of him yet. No matter what, she'd hurry home. She wanted to be near Ethan.

She swung open the kitchen door and sniffed appreciatively. "Scones," she whispered to Jonah. "We're in luck."

But one look at her mother, sitting at the scarred kitchen table and looking exhausted, pierced Cleo's good mood. She hurried over. "What's wrong, Mama?"

Jasmine pulled a mug out of a cabinet even as she sent Cleo a worried look. "What else? Another nightmare."

Cleo swallowed, looking from her mother to her sister, then back again. Celeste's skin looked paper-thin and pale, shadows circling her normally bright eyes. Her heart sinking, Cleo dropped into the chair beside her. "Mama, this has gone far enough. We need to do something. Can't you at least tell us what you're dreaming about?"

Jonah cooed, as if in encouragement, and Cleo's fears eased a bit when Celeste held out her arms for the baby. Celeste even smiled a little as she looked into his face and stroked his wisps of blond hair. "I'll be all right, girls. Really."

Jasmine sent Cleo another pointed look as she plopped a mug of hot coffee in front of her. "If you ask me, we can blame those damn reporters and all their questions about the skeleton."

Cleo noticed her mother stiffen. She took a fortifying gulp of Jasmine's miraculous coffee and then put all the steel she could muster into her voice. "Mama, what's bothering you? We're not going to let up until you tell us."

Celeste settled Jonah closer against her and slid her own mug of coffee toward the table's center so the baby couldn't reach it. "I don't know whether to blame the reporters or not, but I did have the nightmare again last night." She sighed, and it was a sad, weary sound. "And Blanche was in the dream."

Cleo and Jasmine exchanged glances. Their mother had never talked in detail about the nightmare before. "She, um, hasn't been in it before?"

Celeste shook her head. "No. I realize that now. Before last night it had always been the same. My brother Jeremiah…carrying someone I always assumed was my sister. But last night I knew it couldn't be Blanche."

Cleo swallowed another gulp of coffee, unsure what to say next. Should Celeste be talking of it at all? Would that only make it seem more real? But God knew that bottling it up inside her hadn't given her any relief. "How was the nightmare different last night, Mama?"

"I've always been alone, watching Jeremiah come toward me. I'm always…dreading what he holds in his arms and he's always insisting that I obey him and look at it."

An icy finger dragged down Cleo's spine and she saw Jasmine shiver, too.

"But last night…" Celeste continued. "…last night I wasn't alone. Blanche was on the shore beside me, as young and beautiful as ever, and she spoke to me."

Jasmine slipped into the chair beside Cleo. Cleo saw that her sister was trembling, and underneath the table she slipped her hand over her sister's and squeezed reassuringly. Celeste often said that Jasmine was an "old soul." Whether that was true or not, it was clear that Jasmine's soul, whatever its age, was afraid.

So was Cleo, and she suddenly longed for Ethan.

"Mama," Jasmine started, then stopped, cleared her throat, began again. "Mama, what did Aunt Blanche say to you?"

Celeste's beautiful green eyes looked off into the distance. Cleo felt that icy finger again and chills ran up through her scalp and down to her ankles.

"She told me that the past is about to rise up and greet me." Celeste's voice was reed-thin and eerie-sounding. "She told me to be careful to make the right choices."

The temperature in the kitchen dropped. Or maybe it just seemed that way. But Cleo didn't imagine the charged silence in the room. She didn't know what to say. Jasmine looked just as stunned.

Cleo's yearning for Ethan resurfaced with a force that startled her. She was used to taking care of herself and other people. Was this what one night in his bed could do? She wasn't sure if she liked this need to have him near her.

But then, as if she'd beckoned him to her with the force of her feelings, he walked through the kitchen door. Dressed in jeans and a long-sleeved denim shirt, he looked disgruntled. Their gazes collided and his face hardened. "What's wrong?" he asked. "I woke up and you weren't there."

"I…" Cleo couldn't put her relief into words, and that worried her even more. "I came for some breakfast and…ended up chatting with Mama and Jasmine." She added a falsely casual note to her voice that made it sound as if she hadn't seen any reason to hurry home, even though their relationship had taken a new turn the night before.

"You were chatting," he repeated flatly. He didn't sound very happy.

She shrugged. "You were sleeping." Was she supposed to just start spilling the disturbing details of her mother's nightmare? She wanted to, oh, she did, but the dream was almost as scary as this new need she had for Ethan.

She could feel her mother's and Jasmine's puzzled stares. Obviously they expected her to be more open with her husband. They were the kind of family that shared problems with one another. But Cleo had never fully shared her problems with Ethan, so she avoided looking at them and offered to get him a cup of coffee.

While he served himself instead, Cleo whispered to Jasmine and her mother that they could talk about the nightmare later. For now, she just wanted to smooth over the awkward moment. Some other time, when she had better control of herself and her fears, when she didn't feel so vulnerable, she could tell Ethan all about Celeste's nightmare. About Raven's murder.

But as the awkwardness hung around the kitchen table like a stubborn cloud, Cleo thought it might be best to get out of the B and B altogether. She stood and reached for Jonah, taking the baby out of her mother's arms. "Ready to go, Ethan?"

He stared at her over the rim of his mug. He'd taken maybe three sips of his coffee. "Now?"

She took a step toward the back door and caught sight of her aunt, uncle and cousin Frannie coming through the woods. Uh-oh. It looked like a family powwow in the making, and if it was, Ethan would know she'd been trying to keep things from him. "Now," she said firmly. "I'd like to go home now."

If she became involved in a family discussion of the past, and became scared again, she'd turn toward Ethan for sure. She didn't want to want his support and comfort that much. If she came to depend on him, it might jinx what they could eventually find together. Just as she'd jumped the gun on saying "I love you," she didn't want to jump the gun on needing Ethan.

He looked wary and puzzled and maybe even a little hurt, but she ignored him as she said a cheerful goodbye to her mother and sister. She planned on a just-as-cheerful wave to the Hannons before she and Ethan escaped to their cars.

And they almost made it. Cleo's hand was on the doorknob when Sheriff Rafe Rawlings pushed through the swinging door that led into the kitchen from the dining room. His gaze took in the family group and then he smiled a little as the doorknob was pulled from Cleo's grasp and Yvette, Edward, and Frannie filed into the kitchen.

"I'm sorry to disturb your family, Celeste," he said politely, "but I have some questions for you and Yvette."

That fingernail of fear skittered down Cleo's back again. She instinctively edged closer to Ethan, and she felt his warm palm on her shoulder. Oh, it was so easy, too easy, to lean on him.

She made herself move away. She was the capable, dependable one. "What's this about, Rafe?"

Celeste spoke for him. "It's about Raven." Her eyes roamed the faces of her family. "Get some coffee and sit down, everyone. I think we all need to hear what the sheriff has to say." Ethan moved and she pinned him with her gaze. "That means you, too, Ethan Redford."

More chairs were drawn up, more coffee poured. Cleo found herself at the table between her mother and Ethan. Jonah had drifted off for an unusually early morning nap in her arms. Rafe sat directly across the table and addressed his remarks to Celeste and Yvette, who were positioned beside each other.

"My investigation of Raven Hunter's death has brought me to Blanche and Jeremiah," he said. He reviewed the details of where and when the skeleton had been found, and the bullet, then told about the identification of the remains. As he spoke, Cleo felt Ethan's increasing attention.

"I've been talking with Jackson Hawk and wanted to verify with you what he's told me," Rafe said.

"Jackson Hawk?" Ethan asked.

Rafe answered the question matter-of-factly. "He's an attorney who lives on the Laughing Horse Reservation."

"And a friend of Raven's," Yvette added. "That much I remember."

Rafe turned his gaze her way. "What else do you recall, Yvette? Were you aware of your sister's affair with Raven?"

"Of course." Cleo's aunt nodded. "The three of us sisters were very close, and she needed our help at times to slip away from Jeremiah." Yvette reached out beside her to rub her husband's forearm. "I hadn't met Edward yet, you see, and I had never seen a love like that. It was something you could touch, how they felt about each other, and I thought it wonderfully romantic." A sad smile touched her lips.

Rafe circled his coffee mug with his hands and spoke carefully. "You say that you helped her give Jeremiah the slip. Did he oppose the match?"

Yvette's eyebrows raised. "Didn't Jackson tell you that?"

Rafe was noncommittal. "I want to hear your impressions."

"Jeremiah absolutely opposed the match. He was outspoken in his hatred for Raven, any Native Americans, actually, but particularly Raven." Yvette sighed. "Jeremiah wasn't a tolerant or understanding man, Rafe. I don't know what fueled his hatred, but it was very, very real."

"And you, Celeste?" Rafe switched his gaze to Cleo's mother. "Is that how you remember it?"

Cleo could see her mother's shoulders tense. "It was so long ago, Rafe. I don't have much memory of those times." Confusion clouded her usually beautiful green eyes. "But if Yvette says so..." Celeste shrugged. "I do remember Raven and Blanche, of course, and their love. But what about Raven's younger brother, Storm? He might know something."

Rafe nodded. "We're trying to contact him—both the sheriff's department and Jackson Hawk. But you can't think of anything else, Celeste?"

She slowly shook her head. "I only seem to remember what came after. Of Summer, and what a beautiful little girl she was and then how glad I was to take her into my home and into my life."

Cleo looked down at Jonah, still sleeping in her arms. She'd never doubted her mother's love for her cousin, but with Jonah to care for now she better understood how a woman could take another's child into her life and love it as her own. Without thinking, she looked over at Ethan and caught his gaze on her. There was something, some uncertainty, on his face, and it worried her. But Rafe's next question distracted Cleo.

"The night that Raven disappeared, witnesses spotted him on your brother's property. That was the last place Raven was seen. What do you both remember of that?"

Yvette spoke first. "I wasn't home. I was getting my teaching credential at that time and was in Bozeman. When I came home, Jeremiah told me he'd offered Raven money to leave Blanche, leave Whitehorn." Her face was sad again. "It seemed like something Jeremiah would do, and it made me furious. But the damage had already been done. Raven was gone and Blanche was heartbroken. I concentrated on my sister and dealt with my brother as little as possible."

She turned to her sister. "And Celeste—"

Yvette broke off and no one else spoke as they all looked at Celeste. Her hands were visibly trembling and she stared unseeing into the distance.

"Mama?" Jasmine called, her voice frightened.

Cleo gently touched her mother's shoulder. "Mama, what's wrong?"

"That night…" Celeste said. One hand shook as she reached up to rub her temple. "It all seems confused to me. Everything about that time."

"Don't think about it, then, Aunt Celeste," Frannie said hastily, obviously uncomfortable with Celeste's distress.

But Cleo's mother shook her head. "I don't think that will work, Frannie. Blanche told me so, clearly, last night."

"Blanche?" Rafe questioned quietly.

Jasmine looked at her mother, received a confirming nod, and then turned to Rafe. "Mama has nightmares. Vivid ones that frighten her. Last night, for the first time, Blanche was in Mama's dream."

Cleo avoided Ethan's gaze. She could feel it on her, and feel his sudden understanding that she'd deliberately withheld the truth of the situation from him. Was he relieved or hurt?

"Blanche told me the past was rising up," Celeste said, her voice wavering a bit. "She warned me to make the right choices." She smiled in Frannie's direction, a wan, worn smile. "And I have a feeling not thinking about the past isn't one of the options open to me anymore, Frannie."

Ethan drove Cleo and the baby home from the B and B shortly after Rafe Rawlings left. The sheriff had obviously been unsurprised at the lack of detail Yvette and Celeste had been able to give about events thirty years earlier. Events that appeared to include a murder.

A sweep of cold had run over Ethan the night before when Cleo had whispered "I love you." It had rushed over him again this morning, colder and stronger, when he realized all that she'd been keeping from him in the past few weeks.

Guilt, remorse, and resignation coiled in his gut. He should have been there for her, and yet he doubted he could have given her the support she needed. She had her family for that, if indeed Cleo required anyone's bolstering.

Ethan braked in the driveway of their house and reached for his door handle, but Cleo put her hand on his arm. "I'm sorry. I should have told you what was going on. I don't know why…"

Ethan remembered a night months ago, the night she *had* told him something. She'd told him about her mother's nightmares then, and he'd kept on walking up the stairs, unwilling to get too close to her. Thinking it was best.

"It's okay," he said.

She swallowed. "It's just that you weren't around very much…and you didn't seem that interested in local goings-on, and…" She trailed off again.

He hadn't seemed that interested in her. Or interested enough. Damn. All along he'd been worried he hadn't anything to give Cleo. And he still continued to take, take, take. From her body. He thought of that soft "I love you" again. From her heart.

He squeezed his eyes shut. "It's all right, Cleo. You don't have to explain."

"But I do. Honestly, at first it didn't seem to have anything to do with us, with my family. But then—"

"Then those reporters showed up at Beansprouts yesterday, Cleo." Rafe had mentioned the incident and Ethan had quickly probed for the details. "Maybe I could have helped with that."

She waved away the thought. "They were gone by the time you got there. And I'd already spoken with Jasmine. Everyone was okay."

Except him. Ethan tried to force away the stupid, selfish thought, but it pierced him. Once again he'd had a chance to do something for Cleo, and failed. Once again she'd taken care of things herself.

Worry lines etched her brow and she looked over her shoulder at the baby strapped in his car seat. "Do you think Jonah is okay? He never takes a nap this long." She released her safety belt so she could lean across her seat to put her hand to his cheek. "I think he's a little warm."

But she muttered the words to herself, and Ethan was certain she wasn't soliciting his opinion. In caring for Jonah and everything else, Cleo was perfectly capable. And then there was her family. They'd rally around if necessary. It was his firsthand knowledge of their unequivocal support and caring—he'd seen it in that kitchen just this morning—that made him feel so hellishly inadequate.

And unnecessary.

"I'm heading back to Houston tonight," he said abruptly. The idea came out of nowhere, but it sounded good. Facing Cleo and his own inability to be what she needed—*someone* she needed—made him restless.

Her eyebrows shot up. "What? You just returned yesterday."

He avoided her gaze, looking out the window instead. Through the trees he glimpsed the lake, but its calm waters couldn't soothe him. "There's always something that needs to be done at the office."

He felt her looking at him. "How's the move of your headquarters coming? When do you think you'll be in Whitehorn permanently?" she asked.

His hands squeezed the steering wheel. "It's not that simple," he said. Actually, whatever had been done could be easily *un*done. Perhaps it was better if he left Cleo and Jonah to their life.

The image of his sister jumped into Ethan's mind. *I'm sorry, Della. But I'm doing the best I can here.* He knew she would want him to take care of her son. But he also felt certain she would understand why he found it so hard to become part of Jonah and Cleo's life. When he looked in the mirror, he could never duck the reflection of Jack Redford. The man had been driven by his emotions: if he was despondent he would drink, if he was angry he would yell, if he was frustrated he would hit.

Ethan had always been grateful that he didn't seem to have any emotions at all.

"I'm going to Houston," he said again. Cleo and Jonah would be better off without him. He restarted the car, still refusing to look at her. "Go ahead and get out, Cleo. I have a few errands to run before I make this next trip."

Ten

Cleo doodled on a list pad because she didn't know what else to do with herself. Ethan was still on his errands, Jonah was taking his afternoon nap, and she'd already dusted, vacuumed and scrubbed floors. Bed linens had been changed. But not one of those activities had improved her mood.

She couldn't believe Ethan was leaving again. Last night they'd made love. Today he was running from her.

At the top of her pad she'd written "Things I Should Have Known." An easy list to fill. Beside Item Ten, she'd penned "'Fat free' was too good to be true."

And at the Item One position, of course, she'd written, "Never marry for one-sided love."

So, see, she couldn't blame it on Ethan. He had

never pretended to offer her more than the building that Beansprouts was housed in—and Jonah.

Cleo crumpled her silly list and tossed it into the garbage, then wandered down the hall to Jonah's dim bedroom. Though she hadn't heard a peep from him yet, she still felt the need to check on him. He'd dozed the morning away and was still taking a full-length nap. Inhaling the sweet scent of baby, she leaned against the doorjamb and watched him sleep. Never, never could she regret Jonah in her life.

He was her love, and he could be her happiness.

All she had to do was let go of that little fantasy she'd been hoping to make a dream-come-true with Ethan.

She had to let go of Ethan.

Oh, he'd be there one way or another. Not in her bed or in their child's life, but she had no doubt he'd send regular checks and put in erratic appearances.

But they'd never be a family. She'd have to let go of him…and of that sweet dream.

The shrill ring of the phone broke into her thoughts. Cleo hurried to answer it and then wished she hadn't—because on the other end of the line was Jasmine saying, "We have a small problem."

Cleo groaned. "No. Not another problem. Not today."

"Sorry, sis, but this one actually has your name written all over it." Jasmine hauled in an audible breath. "Jonah's grandparents are here."

"What?" Cleo blinked. "Who? Where?"

"You forgot 'why?'"

Cleo squeezed the phone. *"Jasmine."*

"Okay, okay," her sister relented with a quick laugh. "At the B and B. It's those Houston grandparents you told us about. You know, the ones who precipitated your quickie marriage to Ethan."

"Jasmine," Cleo said again, then instinctively lowered her voice. "Don't call it a quickie marriage. And please tell me they're not standing right there."

"I'm in the office with the door closed. The Covingtons are enjoying tea and cookies in the living room."

The B and B living room. Cleo's stomach twisted. "What do they want?"

"To visit their grandson, they said. Ethan promised them the three of you would visit Houston in the fall, but they apparently couldn't wait. They were driving in this direction to see some friends and decided to make a short detour."

Cleo groaned. "Oh, no."

"Oh, yeah," Jasmine countered cheerfully. "And they're excited about meeting you, the paragon of all womanhood. Ethan must have painted quite a picture. You're just lucky I didn't tell them about the time you whacked off my bangs and gave me permanent-marker freckles."

"I was seven!"

"And I was three. Just remember you owe me, big sister." Jasmine's voice changed from lightly teasing to serious. "And I'm about to collect."

Beads of sweat popped out on Cleo's brow. "What?" she said warily.

"I want them to stay with you."

Cleo could only emit a little moan.

"Don't keel over on me. It's just that we're pretty full here and I don't want to put Mama under any more strain."

Cleo moaned again. Jasmine was right. If Jonah's grandparents stayed at the bed-and-breakfast Celeste would feel obligated to entertain them. She was too exhausted for that.

"I don't know where Ethan is," Cleo said desperately.

"Well, you better find him," Jasmine replied, "because the Covingtons can't wait to get to know your entire little family quite a bit better."

Your entire little family. Cleo's stomach twisted again. That was exactly what the three of them were not. She blotted her damp forehead with her wrist. "Okay, Jasmine, give them directions to our house and tell them we insist they stay with us. But can you stall them for a bit? Maybe Ethan will get home soon. We'll need a little time to get our act together."

As she hung up the phone, she almost laughed

out loud at her last words. Get their act together. Oh, yeah. Everything about their marriage was an act.

And for the Covingtons, who had given up their fight for Jonah because she'd become Ethan's bride, it better be a darn good one.

In the end, Jasmine hadn't been able to stall long enough. The first car to pull into Cleo's driveway was not Ethan's Range Rover, but an unfamiliar, expensive sedan. Cleo pasted on what felt like a sick smile, then walked outside to greet the older couple, Jonah in her arms.

Was Ethan going to be surprised when he returned.

If he returned.

At the horrible thought, she widened her smile and reached out a hand to the silver-haired woman and then her stooped but vigorous-looking husband. "I'm Cleo M—Redford," she said, pretending she hadn't almost forgotten her married name. "You must be the Covingtons."

It helped that they were truly friendly and gracious people. Once they brought their few bags inside, the three of them sat in the living room to get acquainted. To Cleo's relief, they told her almost immediately that they were happy to not have the responsibility of raising a baby at their age. They had been willing to adopt Jonah if it was best for him, though.

"But he deserves young people, a young family,"

Mrs. Covington said, a warm smile on her lips as she sat on the couch with Jonah in her arms.

Mr. Covington was somewhat cooler, but even he seemed to approve. "Always liked Ethan, but he's a busy man. Jonah needs a mother. And Ethan could use someone to come home to."

Mrs. Covington beamed. "It was so clear he was taken with you, Cleo, when he came to talk to us in Houston."

Cleo beamed back, hoping to conceal her panic. Oh, yeah. Ethan was so taken with her that she had no idea where he was and whether he'd be back in time for dinner.

Dinner.

Thunk. Thunk. The two syllables dropped into her consciousness like sandbags. She'd been so pre-occupied with housing the Covingtons, she'd hadn't even considered *feeding* them.

Swallowing hard, she rose to her feet. "Would you excuse me for a moment?" She smiled at their immediate assent and dashed for the phone in Ethan's office, the phone farthest away from her guests.

Speed Dial No. 2 was the Big Sky B and B. She had to beg dinner off of Jasmine. No way would the grandparents leave Jonah with a woman who did what Cleo did to food.

For the second time that day a cold sweat broke

out over Cleo's skin. A short conversation with her sister didn't help matters.

She hung up the phone, her heart thrumming. Even the sudden appearance of Ethan in the office didn't bring any relief.

"We're sunk," she told him.

He blinked. "We can't be. I just talked with Ned and Betsy. They like you. And I'm…sorry for leaving like that. But you covered just fine."

All the tension she'd been holding at bay rushed in. Mortified, Cleo felt tears start in her eyes and she covered her face with her hands.

"Cleo."

Shaking her head, she whirled away from him. "I'm fine," she choked.

"You're not." He pulled her toward him and turned her into his arms. "I'm sorry, honey," he said again. "I'm sorry for so many things."

Cleo didn't listen to his words. She only felt the warm comfort of his hands running down her back and his strong heartbeat against her cheek. This was what she'd wanted since going to the B and B this morning—Ethan holding her, Ethan saying it was going to be okay.

But then it struck her again. The knowledge that a hug couldn't make this immediate crisis any better. She stepped away, rubbing her cheeks with the backs of her hands. "We're still sunk," she said.

He frowned. "Cleo, what the hell are you talking about?"

"We need to make a good impression on the Covingtons, right?"

He nodded cautiously. "Right."

"Prove to them what a sweet little family we are, right?"

He nodded again. "Yes."

"And food. A family would need that, right?"

"Uh-huh." He retreated a step, as if he were afraid of what she might do next. "But we have food, Cleo, right? The refrigerator and freezer are full. The cupboards, too."

She moved closer to him and lowered her voice. "That's all for show."

His brow pleated. "Cleo? Are you all right?"

She licked her dry lips. "What would you say if I told you I can't cook, Ethan?"

"You can't cook?" he echoed stupidly.

"Unless you consider instant oatmeal in the microwave, cooking."

"What?" he said.

"I can pour from a box and add milk or pour from a can and add water. But even heating's iffy."

He took another step back. "No," he said. "I don't believe it. Not you."

She nodded. "Believe it. And I tried to cover it tonight like I've done all the other times by begging a Jasmine donation, but she doesn't have a thing for me and was on her way out."

He blinked again and she could see his mind working, going over the meals they'd shared. He blinked once more and she knew he had tallied up all the take-out and leftovers and recipes that Jasmine "desperately needed" them to taste test. His head started shaking slowly from side to side.

"I'm sorry, Ethan," Cleo whispered. "But unless it's cornflakes or chicken noodle soup, we're *Titanic*-level sunk."

He ignored her apology to attack the cuffs of his denim shirt. With quick movements, he rolled them up his strong forearms.

Cleo eyed his determined movements. "What are we going to do?"

"We're going to start being more honest with each other, Cleo."

She was afraid to ask, but she had to. "What's that mean?"

"It means, lucky for Ned and Betsy—unless they like instant oatmeal, of course—that *I* can cook."

Cleo's knees went weak. "You can cook? Really?"

"Really. How does pasta primavera sound?"

"Like music to my ears," she said, still stunned. Ethan Redford, consummate deal-maker, could *cook?* "I could kiss you."

Ethan turned toward the door. "Maybe we should start being honest about that, too," he said.

* * *

By the time the pasta primavera had been pre-pared and consumed, Cleo found she could relax, even with Betsy Covington keeping her company in the kitchen as she put the last of the dishes away.

Cleo hugged to herself the knowledge that, at least for tonight, she and Ethan had achieved a real partnership. As he'd made the meal, he'd smiled to himself often—she had the distinct feeling he was still bemused by her own admitted clumsiness in the kitchen—but they'd worked together well. Under his direction, she'd put together a passable green salad, though his lips had twitched at the sight of her inele-gant carrot chunks.

He'd touched her, too. She shivered now, remem-bering it. His shoulder and hip rubbing against her to make room for himself at the countertop. A light swat on her behind to move her aside when her tip-py-toe stretch still couldn't reach the water pitcher in the highest cupboard. His fingers lingering on the small of her back as he untied her apron before politely pulling out her chair.

Around the table itself, they'd been in perfect concert, too. He prompted her to tell the Covingtons tales of life at the day care center and she showed her interest in Ethan's business by following up some of Mr. Covington's questions with a couple of her own.

Now from the living room came the low murmur

of the men's voices. Both men sat on the couch and Jonah's grandfather was feeding the baby his evening bottle. Mrs. Covington paused with a dish towel in her hand, peering through the kitchen doorway at the sight the three made. She smiled softly.

"Oh, look," she said.

Cleo did. Jonah was nestled in the crook of his grandfather's arm, but the baby's eyes were fixed on Ethan. They stared at each other, unblinking, and then the baby's mouth quirked around the nipple, sending a sweet, hopeful smile Ethan's way. Cleo's heart clenched. And then again, when Ethan surprised her by returning the smile to Jonah.

It was unexpected and just as sweet as the baby's, and maybe it was her imagination, but she thought she saw hopefulness in Ethan's smile, too.

Her spirits, already buoyed by the success of dinner, bubbled higher, and the words just popped out. "I love them," she said. Maybe they were going to be a family, after all. Maybe Ethan had just needed time to get used to the idea.

Betsy Covington smiled again and her gaze was warm. "That's what I came to find out. I know Ethan promised you'd visit in the fall, but I couldn't wait that long."

"I understand," Cleo said. Patience wasn't her strong suit, either. But she'd been right not to push things…push Ethan. He'd just needed time to see how things could—should—be with them. She just *knew* he wasn't going to leave again tomorrow, despite what he'd said.

"And to be honest," Betsy continued, "because of the way Ethan and Della were raised, I couldn't stop worrying. I'm surprised how well Ethan is coping with instant parenthood."

A little chill ran down Cleo's spine. She didn't know much about the way Ethan and his sister had been raised. He had been so closemouthed about it, only a few hints about growing up on the wrong side of the tracks and about his less-than-warm father.

"Ethan would do anything for Jonah," Cleo said.

"Even marry."

Cleo inhaled a sharp breath, but the other woman put out her hand. "I don't mean it as a criticism, dear, believe me. My own son failed Della and he failed his child. Any choices—and changes—Ethan has made for Jonah only deserve my praise."

The resigned hurt in Betsy Covington's face made Cleo search for a safer subject than Jonah's biological father. "You knew Della?"

"Oh, yes." She smiled sadly. "Della and my son were engaged at one time. I thought she would be his salvation. I prayed for it, because she was a wonderful person. Despite the disadvantages of her childhood, she was an engaging, optimistic young woman."

Cleo swallowed. That was the second time the older woman had brought up Della's and Ethan's childhood. While part of Cleo didn't want to pry into her husband's past, another part thought knowing what he seemed so reluctant to speak about might cement their fragile, brand-new closeness. She swallowed again. "Ethan doesn't talk much about…his family."

Betsy nodded. "Della always said her brother tried to ignore things that hurt. By refusing to acknowledge his feelings, he could protect himself."

Cleo busied herself wiping an already-clean countertop. "It sounds like Della knew Ethan well."

"Oh, she did. And she adored him. He shielded her from much that went on in their household. But from what I gathered, they lived with a volatile father whose mood swings were exacerbated by drink and a mother who did nothing to help her children or herself."

"Ah." Cleo's fingers gripped the sponge tighter. "And there were…money problems."

Betsy nodded. "And with that in his background, too, it isn't surprising that Ethan has such a drive for making money. That's one of the things that has worried me about leaving Jonah in his care."

Cleo turned around, surprised. The Covingtons appreciated money, too. It was obvious in the enormous solitaire on Betsy Covington's finger, in her impeccable manicure and in the sleek cut of her expensive country-club clothes. "You're worried about Ethan's success?"

"About what he's willing to give up for it." Betsy looked steadily at Cleo. "I've met men like that before. Men who only offer money and not emotion."

Men who only offer money and not emotion. The words dropped, each one ice-cold, into Cleo's brain. Ethan had offered her Beansprouts. He said he would always provide for her and the baby. "He wants to take care of Jonah," she said, trying to ignore the sick sense of panic rising in her belly.

"I'm certain of it," the older woman said. "But he needs you to show him how."

Cleo turned away again. Betsy Covington didn't mean Ethan needed Cleo to show him how to diaper the baby or to feed the baby, or to even play with the baby. She meant that Ethan needed Cleo to show him how to love Jonah.

And, of course, Cleo wanted Ethan to love her, too. That little balloon of happiness she'd been floating on slowly deflated. She had no idea how to make it happen.

The Covingtons didn't stay up much later than Jonah. They claimed a desire to rise early in the morning to get started on the next leg of their trip, which would take them into Canada to visit some longtime friends. After pleasant good-nights were exchanged, the older couple drifted down the hall.

With a cup and saucer in each hand, Cleo rose.

Ethan immediately followed, carrying the others. In the kitchen, she placed hers on the countertop. "Go ahead and set them here," she said, not looking at him. "I'll wait for the dishwasher to finish and then unload it and put these in."

"Do it in the morning," he said. It wasn't a suggestion.

Cleo fussed with the cups and saucers, setting each one precisely in the middle of a square tile. "No. I think I'll do it tonight."

"You don't want to go to bed?"

"Mmm." Cleo turned all the cup handles in the direction of the sink and avoided the question. The issue of bed was the last of the evening's hurdles, and she wasn't even sure Ethan realized that it loomed in front of them. The house had four bedrooms. One was used as his office. One was the master bedroom. One was Jonah's. One was the one she'd been using…and was now occupied by their guests. In the short time she'd had before their arrival she'd managed to shuffle a few of her things into Ethan's room.

Yet while she and Ethan had shared his bed last night, all the events of today hadn't made it clear that he'd welcome her back in it again.

There was all she'd held back from him about the skeleton. There was his expressed desire to leave again the next day. There was the strain of the Covingtons' visit. He knew, now, that she didn't cook.

And Cleo knew that his sister Della had thought Ethan ignored his feelings as a way of protecting himself. Betsy Covington wondered if he was the kind of man who offered money instead of emotion.

"Cleo…" Ethan's hand touched her shoulder.

Heat ribboned down her arm.

If that were true, who was going to protect her?

She refused to turn around. "What?" she asked hoarsely.

"Let's go to bed." His hand tightened on her shoulder.

There was a darkness, an intent, in his voice and in his touch that set her heart rattling in her chest. She licked her lips, stalling to get control of its wild movements. Practical, sensible Cleo couldn't be so aroused by a hand, by a voice.

"Maybe I'll, uh…maybe your office—"

"No." His other hand closed around her other shoulder.

Heat streaked down that arm and her fingertips tingled. She wasn't certain he knew what she was talking about. Wiggling her fingers to ease the strange sensation in them, she tried again. "You see, the Covingtons, uh…my room—"

"Cleo." Ethan jerked her back against him, so her shoulder blades hit the hard plane of his chest. He was hot. So hot. "Shut up."

Her eyes squeezed shut. "But the bed—"

"Our bed. We're going to—" now he hesitated "—sleep in *our* bed."

That tingling was racing around her body now. Cleo tried to think of another protest—one last attempt to protect herself—but he threw all hopes of her protest away by curving her hair behind one ear and whispering against it. "I think I missed a few spots last night."

"Missed a few spots?" she echoed stupidly, her mind distracted by the hard press of his body against her bottom.

"Like right here." He swept her hair off her nape and pressed a wet, openmouthed kiss on that surprisingly sensitive skin.

A little helpless noise made it through Cleo's tight throat.

His mouth was back at her ear again. "What was that?" His hard, big arm clamped around her middle, which was a good thing, because all the bones below her waist were ragdoll-soft. "Did you say you want me to kiss you there again?"

She wanted him to kiss her anywhere. Everywhere.

He seemed to figure out she was incapable of answering, because he stopped talking and just started kissing. The back of her neck, the side of her neck, her ear, her throat, every inch of skin he exposed as he unbuttoned her blouse.

As he pulled the sides open, Cleo's eyes drifted open. They were in his bedroom. On his bed.

She couldn't remember the journey from kitchen to mattress.

And when he bent over her to wet with his tongue the silky material of her bra, right over her nipple, she didn't care. Sensible, practical Cleo decided that some details were extraneous.

And some details were delicious.

Ethan explored her body with excruciating slowness. When she tried to reach for him, he firmly placed each hand on one side of the wide pillow beneath her head. "Hold here, honey," he said, and then bent to her skin again, to run his mouth over each of her ribs, to circle her navel with his tongue, to stroke his fingers from hipbone to hipbone.

"Ethan," she whispered, his name coming out more like a moan.

But he wasn't swayed by the plea in her voice, and only settled himself alongside her. He was still completely dressed, and the scratch of his clothes against her skin was erotic.

"Ethan," she tried again, and lifted a hand toward his chest.

He caught it and pulled it back to the pillow. "Hold here," he commanded once more.

She obeyed, because then he sucked her nipple into his mouth and she couldn't do anything but ride the ripples of pleasure that slid down her body, heating her center. Her legs moved restlessly, and Ethan immediately insinuated one hand between them.

They instinctively parted, and then he was between her thighs, his shoulders pressing against the sensitive skin inside them. Cleo gripped the corners of the pillow. "You're still wearing your clothes," she said desperately.

He was looking at her. Cleo's body suffused with a new degree of heat. The silvery moonlight was beaming through their window, making it easy for her to see him. See Ethan, fully dressed, fully between her splayed thighs, looking at her.

Then he shuddered. Cleo saw it roll down his spine, felt his fingers tighten on her hips.

She closed her eyes, even more desperate now. "Ethan. Please. Make love to me."

His fingers tightened again, but he didn't move. "I am, Cleo." And then he bent his mouth to that hot, melting, most intimate spot on her body.

Oh. Cleo jerked. Ethan licked again. Cleo jerked again, her body nearly rising off the bed.

He lifted his head for just a moment. "Hold on," he said.

But she didn't know if he was talking to her or to himself, because when he bent to kiss her again he tightened his grip on her hips and tilted her body. His mouth found her once more, a sweet, sweet spot, and Cleo squeezed the pillow corners to keep herself from shooting straight into the moonlit night and a mind-blowing climax.

But Ethan wanted it all. He wouldn't stop, didn't seem to want to stop. Cleo couldn't catch her breath. Her nipples tightened, swirling into harder points. Desperately close and determined to tell him to stop, she looked down once more.

And just then, Ethan traced one hand down her hip to slide two fingers inside her.

Cleo died.

They used to call it that, the little death, and Cleo understood it now, because her body spasmed and her mind spun free from reality and heaven was certainly the moon-gilded Ethan as he quickly shed his clothes and joined their bodies.

Finally, when both their breathing had quieted, Cleo allowed herself to stroke his hair. Her fingers drifted through it slowly, and she gloried in the freedom to touch him. From the beginning, she had always wanted so much to touch him. Satisfaction and happiness welled up inside her.

She was free to touch him. He was her husband. He was hers.

She spoke without thinking. "Ethan, I—"

His hand quickly covered her mouth. "Shh."

Cleo froze. She wouldn't have believed his sated body could move so quickly, but it must have been an almost reflex that made him stifle her with such speed.

An instinctive reflex.

To protect himself from what she'd been about to say.

Her eyes squeezed tightly shut. She made herself breathe. Then she puckered her lips and kissed away his silencing fingers.

And *then* she stared into the moonlit darkness and listened to the man she loved breathe a sigh of relief when she didn't tell him so.

Eleven

Standing in the front doorway, Cleo lifted her hand for one more wave to the departing Covingtons, then slid a look at Ethan. "How do you think the visit went?"

His brows rose in surprise. "Fine." His lips twitched. "And your coffee and bagels and cream cheese weren't even half bad this morning."

Cleo looked away. Making breakfast had been her excuse for rising earlier than usual. When she'd opened her eyes and met Ethan's across the pillow this morning, she'd been desperate for a reason to escape.

He didn't want her love.

He didn't want her to need him.

And lying beside him in bed, she thought it might

be too easy for him to see that she *did* love him, that she *did* need him. Wildly.

But he'd married her because she was sensible, practical and capable. He'd married her because she was a woman who could handle herself and the adorable baby he'd brought into her life.

As if she'd woken him by her thoughts, in his crib down the hall, Jonah started to cry. Cleo turned quickly, frowning. Usually Jonah took at least an hour's nap in the morning, but she'd put him down only fifteen minutes before.

"Cleo."

Ethan's voice made her pause. "Hmm?" She turned and directed her gaze in the vicinity of his left shoulder, not trusting herself to look at his face without giving her feelings away.

"I just wanted you to know I'm taking a late afternoon plane."

Cleo's heart dipped, and she swallowed. "Okay." Before her expression could give away her disappointment, she turned back toward Jonah's room.

"Cleo."

She slowed, but didn't turn around this time. "What?"

"Are you going to be okay…with the baby?"

His hesitation asked her more. Was she going to be okay with the baby *and* with the limits he was putting on their relationship? No.

But Cleo had her pride. And she was that practical, sensible, capable woman he had married. "Of course," she said, continuing on to Jonah's room. If she wasn't okay now, well, then, she would be. She'd find a way to live with half a marriage. Somehow.

Jonah's face was flushed and he didn't immediately stop crying when she picked him up. A niggle of unease rolled down Cleo's spine. He was usually such an easygoing baby.

She went through the checklist. His diaper was dry and his tummy was full. The worry getting stronger now, she shifted him in her arms and put his cheek against hers. He was hot.

To the tune of his fretting, she carried him into the adjoining bathroom to retrieve the thermometer. Blessing the inventor who thought up something so simple as taking a temperature via the ear, she quickly checked Jonah's.

Well over 98.6.

Clamping down on a strange nervousness—at Beansprouts they handled kids with temperatures weekly!—Cleo reached for the infant pain-reliever drops. Squinting at the dosage while she tried to soothe the baby, Cleo considered calling Ethan in to help.

But he'd hired—no, married—her for her experience. She could do this, even though she suddenly realized that she was not quite as calm and cool as when a Beansprouts's kid was sick or injured. "Oh, Jonah," she whispered, putting down the drops to run her hand over his wispy hair. "You're mine now, and I want to make you feel better so badly."

With new resolve, Cleo unwrapped the tamper-proof bottle of medication and filled the dropper with the proper dosage.

Jonah batted her hand away, though, and the dropper fell into the sink. "Okay, okay," she whispered, shifting the baby to her other shoulder. She fished the dropper out, cleaned it, then sucked medicine inside it again, all the while trying not to worry over Jonah's unhappy snuffling.

This time she was ready for his hands. She avoided their reach, and quickly squeezed the medication into his mouth. He blinked, hiccuped, and then some of the sticky red stuff dribbled out of his mouth and onto her sleeve.

Cleo stared down in dismay at the stain on her sleeve, trying to judge how much he'd actually swallowed. But then Jonah started crying again, harder now, and Cleo gave up. Her hair was damp, her hands sticky, and her uneasiness was back, big-time.

She gently cradled Jonah against her, as much for his comfort as for her own. "It's okay, baby," she whispered over and over. She paced the room, patting his back and crooning.

"Okay, okay, okay." That's what she'd promised Ethan. She would be okay. Jonah would be okay. *Please*.

Whether it was thanks to the medicine or thanks

to her pacing, in a few minutes Jonah dropped off again. Cleo carefully put him back in his crib, but she stood over it, watching him sleep.

"Is everything all right?" a low voice suddenly asked in her ear.

Cleo jumped and goose bumps trickled down her back. "You scared me," she whispered accusingly.

Ethan was watching Jonah. "He's quiet now. I came to see if you needed help earlier, but you were walking back and forth and he looked ready to sleep. I didn't want to disturb him."

"He's a little warm," she said, continuing to watch Ethan watch Jonah. There was something on his face, a yearning, maybe, that she'd never detected before.

His hand reached out, but stopped short of touching the baby's blond hair. He minutely adjusted the light blanket covering the baby. "Is it something to be concerned about?"

Cleo didn't want it to be. "No. I'm sure it's nothing," she said, keeping her voice very low. "He could be teething. I gave him some medicine, though."

"Good." His gaze stayed fixed on the baby.

"He looks like you," Cleo found herself saying. She'd noticed it before, but had never expressed it to Ethan. "Not just the coloring, but the shape of his eyes and his mouth."

"You think so?" Ethan's lips quirked in an almost

smile. "Della and I looked quite a bit alike, so maybe it's not so surprising."

He hadn't mentioned his sister in a long time. But Della had been on Cleo's mind a lot, especially since Mrs. Covington had talked about her. "Is that who Jonah gets his sunny disposition from, Della?"

Ethan shot her a glance. "Well, I don't think you could claim that about me, could you?"

Cleo shifted her gaze to the baby again. "Oh, I don't know. You can be very charming. But you know that."

"Charming." Ethan's voice held humor as he ran a slow finger down Cleo's cheek. "I like that."

Her face heated. "It's the deal-maker in you, don't you think?"

"Maybe." The amusement left his voice. "Though that makes me sound shallow."

Cleo shook her head. "You're not shallow, Ethan. Never that. But…contained, I guess is the word." He had walls around him that she wasn't sure could ever be breached. Or that *she* could breach, anyway. Maybe some other woman.

Ethan cleared his throat. "Della used to tell me I was a cold fish."

Cleo couldn't help herself. "Well, *that* I know is not true."

His gaze jumped to hers. She raised her eyebrows, meeting the incredible blue without flinching.

He shook his head, then chuckled. "You surprise me sometimes."

Cleo let it go at that. But maybe that was what she needed to do more often. Surprise him.

After a few more moments Ethan wandered away to complete his packing and make a few phone calls. Without acknowledging how worried she was, Cleo remained by the baby's bedside. When he woke up thirty minutes later, Cleo instantly put down her book and rose from the rocking chair.

He was hardly fretting at all; as a matter of fact he appeared more listless than she'd ever seen him. Cleo took the baby in her arms, and knew instantly that his temperature had risen.

She swallowed a bubble of panic. She forced down the instant urge to call out for Ethan.

He would be leaving for the long drive to the airport shortly. She would just call the pediatrician, make an appointment and get her fears calmed by a professional.

Keeping her arms protectively around Jonah, she headed for the kitchen and her address book.

But her fears were escalated instead of soothed when the nurse who answered the phone insisted Cleo come in immediately. High temperatures for infants under a year old could be particularly dangerous, the woman explained.

Cleo felt strangled. She could hardly get out

enough breath to finish the phone call. "Ethan!" she called.

His brow furrowed, he appeared in the kitchen. "What's the matter?"

Cleo opened her mouth, then closed it. He was wearing one of his deal-maker suits and, as usual, it added another layer to that protective wall of his. Mentally forcing down her panic, she spoke again, more quietly. "I just wanted you to know I'm taking Jonah to the doctor. His fever seems to be getting worse."

Ethan frowned. "I don't like the sound of that."

Cleo wanted to scream that she didn't, either, but there wasn't any reason to worry Ethan. That was her job, to calmly, practically, capably, handle these kinds of minor crises. That's why he'd married her. "It'll be okay," she said firmly.

His gaze raked her face, and she struggled to keep it composed. "You're sure?"

Cleo's stomach was flip-flopping with nervousness, but she refused to let him see it. "I'm sure," she said. "I'll just put a few things in the diaper bag and be on my way."

In Jonah's room, she had to put the baby in the crib to restock the bag with diapers and an extra outfit. She breathed deeply of the baby-powder scent of the room, trying to calm herself, but when she couldn't seem to unzip the bag, Cleo realized her hands were shaking. Shaking hard.

She bit down on her lower lip, scolding herself. She was good in emergencies, darn it. Everybody said so. It had always been so.

At the sound of Jonah's little whimper, she rushed over and picked him up again. But she'd never had her own child. His overheated skin and listless gaze scared the heck out of her.

She'd never had her own sick child.

Only by admonishing herself to focus, could Cleo get herself and the baby ready. With Jonah in her arms and the diaper bag slung over her shoulder, she hurried down the hall to the kitchen. "Keys," she said softly to the baby. "We just have to find my keys and then we can get you some help, sweetheart. Mommy's going to take very good care of you."

Cleo's keys were missing from their convenient little hook. Her stomach roiled as she tried to think of where they could be. In another panic, she whirled.

To face Ethan. There was a tight expression on his face. "I'll drive you," he said.

Drive her! She almost sank to the floor with gratefulness. But no. A capable, practical woman wouldn't need to be driven to a doctor's appointment. "I'll be fine," she said. Of course she would be.

His mouth tightened. "For God's sake, for once—" He stopped, his voice quieting. "Cleo, you're shaking all over. I'm not letting you drive… our son."

Our son. Cleo wanted to think about those words, but her worry was taking over again. Ethan steered her toward the door and she realized he was right. Her whole body was trembling, and continued to tremble for the entire drive to the doctor's office.

In the back of Ethan's Range Rover, Cleo sat next to Jonah's car seat, so that she could stroke the baby's arm, his hand, his hair. "I love you," she whispered.

She prayed, too.

Ethan hated hospitals. He hated the smells and the lights and the quiet soles on the nurses' shoes. The last time he'd been in one was to say goodbye to his sister.

And now his sister's son was in another antiseptic, bright and too quiet hospital room.

It had all happened so damn quickly. He and Cleo had taken Jonah into the pediatrician's examining room. The nurse had taken his temperature. Then the doctor had hurried in and quite calmly, matter-of-factly, told them to drive to the hospital. He would call ahead so they would be ready for Jonah.

When babies had temperatures as high as Jonah's, the pediatrician had explained it could be a sign of a bacterial infection that could lead to…Ethan couldn't even wrap his mind around what could happen.

Once at the hospital, some of Jonah's spinal fluid had been immediately drawn. Now they would have to wait for the results. The cultures that would specify the seriousness of the illness would take three days to develop. In the meantime, Jonah would remain in the hospital and be treated with antibiotics in case it was bacterial. The only comforting thing to remember was that this practice was standard.

The walls of the hospital room were painted cream and green. The linoleum floor was a darker green. Jonah appeared small and fragile lying in a stainless-steel crib.

"It looks like a cage," Ethan muttered. When Cleo didn't respond, he turned his head toward her. A green rocking chair sat to one side of the crib. She had slid into it earlier, but she wasn't rocking. Perched on the edge of the seat, she stared in front of her, unseeing.

Something cold and sharp pierced Ethan's chest. "Cleo?"

Her eyes flickered, and then she focused on him. "What?"

Her eyes were like amethyst crystals. For a moment he imagined he could look clear through them, straight into her soul, straight into—

He shook himself. "Do you want me to call someone? Your mother or your sister?"

Her eyes were unfocused again, but she managed to shake her head. "Not now. Not yet."

"God," he muttered, looking away from her face. "It's cold in here." But even colder was the chill in his blood. Cleo was still shaking, finely trembling all over, and watching her was almost worse than watching Jonah.

With a smothered oath, he shrugged out of his suit jacket and strode over to drop it around Cleo's fragile shoulders. When she didn't move, he tugged up the collar and brought the edges close together. "There," he said firmly.

There. He'd done what he could for her now. Provided for her.

With two strides he crossed the small room and stood beside the narrow window, staring out over the parking lot and into a small slice of the Montana sky. He tried to focus on his current project. He tried to dredge up the list of calls he knew he needed to make.

He tried damn hard to detach himself from the scene behind him. The child in the hospital crib. The woman in the rocking chair.

Instead, he turned around. Instead, he watched them for hours, as day darkened into night. Nurses and doctors bustled in and out. Jonah woke up, Cleo fed him a bottle, Jonah went back to sleep, Cleo went back to staring in front of her. And trembling.

Always trembling.

He didn't know exactly what time it was, but it

was fully dark when Cleo finally looked at him. "It's late," she said, and there was surprise in her voice.

Ethan left his place by the window and approached her. "Do you need something? We haven't eaten." He hadn't even thought about it. "Can I—"

Cleo shook her head. "I'm not hungry."

"What about coffee?" Hell, he wanted to do *something*.

Jonah whimpered. Cleo's head whipped around and they both rushed to the crib. When the baby saw them bending over him, his mouth moved into a little smile.

Another cold and sharp pain stabbed Ethan's chest.

Cleo took him up in her arms. "What a good boy," she said. She put her cheek against his hair. "Mommy's good boy."

Ethan looked away. He didn't know why. As Cleo murmured to the baby, he retreated to his spot by the window. More time passed and Jonah must have fallen asleep again because Cleo put him down in the crib.

A nurse came in on her quiet shoes and checked on the baby, then someone else brought in a narrow cot. "For the mama," the man said with a quick smile. On its middle were stacked a thin pillow and a mint-green blanket.

Cleo looked over at Ethan, then slipped his jacket off her shoulders. At some point she'd put her arms through the sleeves and rolled them up. Now she unfolded them, sending him a small, apologetic smile. "Here," she said, holding it out to him. "Thank you."

It wasn't any warmer in the hospital room. At least it wasn't to him. "Keep it," he said.

She shook her head. "I'm going to use the blanket." She pointed at the cot. "Why don't you go on home?"

Go on home. That was a good idea. He could go into his office. Fire up the laptop. Do some work. Send some faxes. Check his e-mail.

Anything to forget about Jonah in his stainless-steel cage and Cleo, with her amethyst-crystal eyes and her shivering body. He opened his mouth. "No" came out.

Her brows came together. "Why not? You could get some rest."

A very definite no. Hell. The last thing he'd be able to do was go to that bed they'd shared the past two nights and sleep.

A feathery shiver tickled his spine as he remembered the sensation of Cleo's skin against his palms, of sinking into her hot, still climaxing body. He wanted to touch her, taste her again.

He wouldn't go back to that bed until she was there beside him.

"I'll stay right here," he said.

"I can handle it," she said defensively.

Ethan frowned. What did she mean, she could handle it? Hell, he *wanted* her to handle it. He worked best when emotions were at a minimum and, take it from him, hospitals weren't the kinds of places that minimized emotions. But maybe it was because he couldn't get Della out of his mind, or maybe it was because he knew Cleo's eyes would haunt him if he left her here. "I won't be in your way."

She turned away from him wearily, and they retreated to their separate corners. He shifted against the ugly green vinyl chair beneath the window. Cleo curled up on the cot.

Hours went by and neither of them spoke. Jonah slept, thank God. And then so did Cleo.

It was well after midnight when, restless, Ethan found the controls to the television in the corner of the room. He turned it in his direction then thumbed it on—no volume. The flickering images offered him a flat, sterile kind of company.

During the third-in-a-row rerun of episodes of the "I Love Lucy" show, Jonah whimpered. Ethan immediately looked toward Cleo. She didn't move. The baby whimpered again, louder, and Ethan pushed to his feet.

Cleo had looked exhausted *before* they arrived at the hospital. If he could quiet the baby, he guess he'd give it a try.

Over the side of the crib, he peered at Jonah's

face. The baby was looking in the other direction, his eyes open. Then his face screwed up, readying itself for another wail. "Champ," Ethan whispered softly. "Over here, champ."

Jonah's head rolled on the mattress and his expression eased.

"That's right," Ethan whispered. "I'm here, champ." *Champ.* Where the hell had that come from? He'd completely forgotten the pet name Della had called her son.

Jonah whimpered again. Apparently a few words in the night wasn't enough to comfort him. Casting a quick glance to make sure that Cleo was still undisturbed, Ethan scooped Jonah up into his arms. Jonah blinked. Ethan blinked back.

"That's right, champ. The guys are going to handle this one. We're going to let Cleo sleep."

With quiet footsteps he retreated to the window. The two of them looked out on that slice of sky. Ethan counted the stars in their little rectangle of darkness. "Five," he whispered to the baby. "There are five twinkling stars." His gaze snagged on the baby's face and his wide-eyed expression.

He looks like Della. Cleo had said Jonah resembled him, but she hadn't known his sister. Thinking of Della, he felt another stab of that cold pain pierce him, and Ethan sucked in a breath. But the pain didn't subside and he couldn't seem to sidestep it.

He stared down into the baby's face. "Your mama

was special," he whispered. "And I still can't believe she's gone. I always watched out for her, always."

Ethan glanced up at those five twinkling stars. Maybe it was Della's turn now. He gathered the baby closer and squeezed shut his eyes. *Watch over him, sis. Watch over Cleo, too.*

Watch over the three of us.

Ethan breathed easier after that. Jonah fell asleep against his chest, and he reluctantly laid him back in his crib, thinking the baby might have a more comfortable rest. Soon after, Cleo stirred, and through slitted eyelids he watched her get up to check on the baby.

She stood by the baby's crib for almost an hour. Ethan thought about telling her to lie back down. He thought about joining her. But instead he watched her. Her hands gripped the top rail of the crib and she took in long breaths.

His chest ached again, damn it. Ethan tried avoiding the hurt by avoiding the sight of Cleo. He closed his eyes.

Watch over her, he told Della again.

Suddenly it was morning.

He blinked, stretched, his muscles as stiff as an overbaked pretzel. Jonah slept.

Cleo was in the rocker again. Somehow, in the hours since he'd last looked at her, she'd turned even more fragile. Shadows darkened her eyes. He knew if he touched her she'd still be shaking and cold.

That unfamiliar pain twisted inside him again. He rose and walked toward her. "Cleo—"

"You're awake." She popped up, her movements jerky. "Will you watch Jonah? I'll be right back."

He stared at her. She was talking fast, moving fast, clearly fueled by nerves. "Of course."

"The doctor should be here in an hour or so. The nurse just checked Jonah. No change."

No, all the changes were to Cleo. Her cheekbones poked against skin almost translucent with weariness. No doubt, with the exception of that brief nap, she hadn't slept the rest of the night. On her way to the door she halted at the cot and frowned. With another jerky movement, she snatched up the blanket, shook it out, then folded it into a precise square.

Ethan stared at her. The blanket had already been folded into a precise square. Cleo was strung so tight he could practically hear her tendons humming.

"Cleo—"

But he was speaking to her back, and then the door.

She must have run downstairs and then back up, she was back in such short order. In one palm she cradled two cups of coffee, a bag from the hospital gift shop in the other.

"Here," she said, shoving the coffees in his direction.

He grabbed both, fairly sure that worry was the only stimulant she needed right now.

She dropped the bag onto the seat of the rocking chair. Out came a teddy bear. Three books. A toy airplane. A build-it-yourself model of a race car. Ethan squinted. He thought the age level said over eight.

More stuff came out of the bag and she arranged it around the room. The only thing she put near the baby was the soft teddy bear, and even that took eleven tries for her to find exactly the right location and pose.

Then she swung around and found him with the coffees. Before he could protest, she grabbed one and a napkin he'd found on the room's tiny table. The coffee went down in one gulp.

She tossed the cup into the trash, then took the napkin and blotted her hands. Next, she used the napkin to wipe down the small table. Then the arms of the rocking chair.

Ethan set his coffee cup down. "Cleo," he said softly.

She pretended she didn't hear him. Or maybe she just couldn't stop her frenetic cleaning.

"Cleo." He approached her, and still she bustled around the room.

With a sigh, he grabbed her by the upper arms. "Cleo," he said, shaking her gently. "Stop. You need to stop, honey."

She looked up at him, the woman who had

become his wife. There were so many things in the amethyst facets of her eyes. Worry, fear, love for the child that he'd come to her with.

That pain tore through his chest, no small stab, but a huge hole. Then something swelled to fill it, something like a heart, and it kept getting bigger.

Cleo's mouth trembled. "I'm scared," she whispered brokenly.

A lump rose in Ethan's throat. His chest hurt, his throat hurt, he never knew there was this much pain in all the world. "I know, honey." He pulled her against his chest.

She broke down then, sobbing against him. He held her tightly, feeling the tension drain from her. "I'm so scared," she said again.

Ethan stared out the window as he stroked her hair. The five stars were gone and it was another sunny day in Montana. He leaned his cheek against the top of her head, breathing through the pain that came in beats now, beats that matched the thudding rhythm of the heart he'd forgotten he had.

The sun was climbing. Its brightness stung his eyes and he blinked away the irritating tears.

Twelve

Later that morning, Ethan made a phone call to enlist the help of Cleo's mother and sister. They arrived at the hospital around noon and, after much coaxing, were able to drag Cleo away for lunch.

Leaving Ethan with a baby that suddenly seemed better. The nurse had said his temperature was down a degree, which only seemed to make Jonah cranky. Ethan took him up into his arms and the two of them paced around the room, inspecting anything the least bit noteworthy.

To the tune of the baby's whimpers, they examined their minute view from the window and the box holding the car model. When neither distracted Jonah, Ethan "flew" the plane over to the crib and retrieved the soft teddy bear. He settled the stuffed toy against Jonah's chest and the baby stopped his fractious wriggling and smiled.

Ethan felt like a million bucks.

He sank into the rocking chair with Jonah and the teddy bear. One foot flat on the floor, he rocked the three of them in a soothing rhythm. At first it seemed that Jonah might protest again, but then Ethan started talking too. He told Jonah about the day he was born. He told him how sad he'd been when Della died. He told him about the vow he'd made at his sister's side. That no one he loved would ever be taken from him again.

He stared down, into his nephew's—his son's—wide blue eyes. "That's right. I love you, champ." He swallowed. "I love you, son."

Jonah's hand reached out and patted Ethan's chin. "That's why I came back to Cleo," he continued. "I wanted the best for you. For us."

The door squeaked as it was pushed open and Ethan lifted his head. Cleo stood framed in the doorway, her mother and sister standing behind her. Her eyes widened. "Is everything okay?"

He nodded, his foot still gently rocking the chair back and forth. "Fine."

She stepped into the room, and his heart clenched. The lunch hadn't made her look any less tired or less fragile. "Do you want me to hold him?" she said hesitantly.

He didn't. But suddenly he realized that Cleo

needed to hold the baby herself. It would comfort her, as strangely, it had comforted him.

He stopped rocking the chair. "Come here," he said, rising from it.

She dashed forward and he gently transferred the baby and the teddy into her arms. Then, just as gently, he pushed her into the rocking chair. From the cot, he fetched the mint-green blanket and unfolded it. Hunkering beside the chair, he carefully tucked the soft fabric around Cleo and Jonah.

With a sigh, she closed her eyes and laid her head against the back of the chair. Ethan stroked her hair off her forehead, then put his hand on the arm of the chair. He pushed, setting it to a very slight rocking.

Celeste spoke quietly from the doorway. "Would you like to go get something to eat now, Ethan?"

He shook his head, his gaze not leaving the faces of the mother and child.

His wife and his child.

As long as they were in the hospital, he wasn't going to leave their sides. He'd always wanted to provide for them, but now they needed something else, too.

They needed his love.

After one more backward look at the baby, Cleo shut Jonah's bedroom door. She rested her forehead on the wood, inhaling a long breath. The past three days were finally over. Jonah was home, and while he was still recovering from a virus, a serious bacterial infection had been ruled out.

A few more days and he'd be completely recovered.

Cleo shivered. She might be able to convince herself the entire episode had been a nightmare, if it wasn't for the chill she couldn't seem to shake and the smell of antiseptic that had found its way into the fiber of her clothes.

She walked into her room and pulled out some fresh clothing and headed for a hot shower. Oh, how she wished she could pretend it had all been a dream. But the truth was, she'd fallen apart. She, who was always so calm in an emergency, who was always so practical under pressure, had cracked.

And Ethan had picked up all the pieces.

He'd picked up Jonah, too.

Under the hot spray of the shower, she remembered walking in on them in the rocking chair that second day. While he'd surrendered the baby readily enough when she'd asked, for the next forty-eight hours Ethan had held the baby as much as she did. He'd also asked intelligent, calm questions of the doctors and the nurses.

He'd brought her tea and soup and wrapped her in blankets when he sensed she couldn't get warm.

The practical, capable, sensible person in that scary, sterile room had been Ethan. In that crisis, he hadn't needed her.

She'd failed him.

Cleo stepped out of the shower, dried off, then pulled on her clothes. She sat on the bed to tie her shoes and thought about just crawling under the covers and going to sleep herself. The sheets were fresh—changed in the hours between the Covingtons's leaving and their departure for the hospital— and maybe in sleep she could avoid the knowledge that was pounding like a bad toothache in her brain.

She'd failed Ethan.

With a sigh, she pushed to her feet. She didn't want to be a coward, too.

In the kitchen she stared at the contents of the cupboards and thought about heating some soup for their dinner. Ethan was in his office, she could hear his printer humming away and his fingers clicking at the keyboard. With another sigh, she turned away from the pantry and looked idly through the small tower of mail and the three-day stack of newspapers.

Three days' worth of front pages focused on Raven's skeleton, his obvious murder and what it would mean to Lyle Brooks's Laughing Horse project. The name Jeremiah Kincaid caught her eye several times.

The past will rise up to meet you. That was the warning Aunt Blanche had sent to her mother in her nightmare. Cleo shivered.

"Are you all right?" Ethan's voice sounded from the entrance to the kitchen.

Cleo looked up, then ducked her head. His golden hair was dark and wet and he smelled like soap. He'd exchanged the deal-maker suit he'd been wearing for three days for a pair of jeans and a sweatshirt, the sleeves pushed up to expose his powerful forearms. She wanted him more than she wanted to be happy.

Because it didn't seem that both could coexist.

"Cleo," he said sharply. "What's going on?"

She gestured vaguely at the newspaper in front of her. "Just catching up on the latest Whitehorn news."

His gaze flicked to the paper, then back to her face. "A sick baby can put a thirty-year-old murder into a little perspective, don't you think?"

"I suppose."

He came forward. "It puts a lot of things into perspective." His fingertips stroked her cheek. "Cleo, honey—"

The phone rang.

Ethan frowned when she stepped away to reach for it. "Let it ring," he said.

Cleo didn't. The person on the other end was Ethan's secretary in Houston. He frowned again as she handed him the receiver.

Hearing one side of the call wasn't easy to avoid, but was easy to understand. Ethan had put his business—*all* his business—on hold for the next few weeks. Though it appeared his secretary was having trouble appeasing some of his clients, Ethan was adamant. He was going to be in Montana spending time with his wife and child.

Cleo shivered again. She didn't blame him for not trusting her anymore, but that feeling of failure rose once more. He'd married her because she could care for Jonah.

The receiver clicked against its cradle. She smelled the delicious fragrance of Ethan as he approached her. His hand ran down the back of her hair. "Now. Where were we?" he said softly.

Cleo knew what she had to do. Had known it from the moment she'd fallen apart in his arms in the hospital room. She whirled to face him. "I won't contest our divorce," she said. Quietly. Firmly. She couldn't believe her voice hadn't broken.

His jaw dropped. "What?"

Cleo swallowed, holding on to her control by just a thread. "I know what kind of marriage we were supposed to have."

His eyes narrowed. "What kind is that?"

"We had a deal. You're very good at arranging those, and I agreed to it."

There was heat in his slitted blue eyes. "I am very good at deals. Maybe too good."

"No!" Cleo wasn't about to lay the blame at Ethan's door. "I went into our marriage with my eyes wide open. I knew that you wanted someone who could keep custody of Jonah for you."

His mouth twisted. "I said something to that effect, didn't I?"

Cleo nodded. "You were completely honest."

"About that—"

"And I want you to know that I was being honest, too. I really thought I could make Jonah a great mother. I am—was—always practical and capable. It's just…just—"

"This time it was your child."

She blinked. He understood. Seeing Jonah in the hospital had made her feel helpless and frustrated, and so very, very afraid.

"Cleo, I didn't like it any more than you did. Seeing Jonah in that hospital crib and thinking something might happen to him was like losing Della all over again."

She looked away. "But you didn't turn into Miss Clean and Tidy." He'd remained calm while her excess nervousness had surfaced in the oddest ways. At one point Ethan had bodily restrained her from remaking the cot for a fifth time. And then there was her small obsession with stacking in alphabetical order the magazines her mother had brought her. *Vanity Fair* always before *Vogue*.

He grinned faintly. "*Mrs*. Clean and Tidy Redford."

Her brows drew together.

That faint grin again. "Just a little name the nurses had for you."

Mrs. Redford. The hospital staff had called her that for three days and she'd felt a fraud each time she'd heard it. She met his gaze squarely. "I'm not holding up to my side of our deal, Ethan. You wanted to continue with your life, your business, while I was supposed to be the caretaker for Jonah."

He shifted uncomfortably. "That's not exactly—"

"You knew I'd fall for Jonah, and I have." She sucked in a breath. "But you deserve to have the kind of wife you wanted. The kind of wife you thought you were getting when we made our deal."

"I wish you'd stop calling it that," he muttered.

Tears stung her eyes. She was going to lose them both, the baby she loved, the man she loved. "So I'll make it easy for us to get a divorce. I'm sure with a little research you or your secretary can find the quickest, simplest manner." A thought struck her. "Maybe because it's been so short a time we could have it annulled."

His jaw was tight and blue fire jumped in Ethan's eyes. "We *have* shared a bed," he said tightly. "Or maybe you've forgotten that?"

At the lethal tone in his voice, Cleo backed up a step. "No, of course not." She'd never forget. All her life she'd remember the hard planes of Ethan's body. Of having him beside her, against her, *inside* her.

"Good." He strode closer.

Cleo stepped away again, the backs of her thighs hitting the edge of the kitchen table. Her heart fluttered at that searing blue in Ethan's eyes. She swallowed. "Ethan—"

He cut her off. "I wish—"

The doorbell rang.

He swore.

Ignoring Ethan's "I wish for once we wouldn't be interrupted," she ran to answer it.

Facing whoever was at the door had to be easier than facing Ethan as they worked out the details of their divorce.

It was her buddy Gil. Cleo was so relieved to see a familiar, friendly face at this moment that she cried out his name with gratitude and immediately stepped into his welcoming embrace.

The past three days had been hell, but watching his wife step into another man's arms—*again*—moments after bringing up divorce stoked Ethan's temper.

"Gil!" Cleo's voice was light and sweet and no one would never know that she'd just torn out his newly discovered heart and fandangoed all over it.

He stood behind her, grim.

Gil squeezed her tight, then pushed her away to kiss her on each cheek, and then lightly on her lips.

Ethan folded his arms across his chest.

The other man blithely ignored him, his eyes only

for Cleo. "I heard you were having a rough time and came by to see if there was anything I could do."

Rough time? Ethan wondered if she was going around Whitehorn complaining about their marriage. Hinting at divorce. God knew that would certainly bring dozens of Cleo's ex-consorts out of the woodwork.

She was beaming up at this one. "I haven't seen you in ages," she gushed. "How have you been?"

Ethan's chest ached. She'd never gushed over him.

"Great. I'm in town visiting Mom and Dad. Had to check on my best girl."

That was it. Ethan stepped forward.

The man's deceptively friendly brown eyes met Ethan's over Cleo's head. "You must be Ethan," he said, his smile too friendly.

Ethan bared his teeth. "The husband."

The man's mouth went instantly serious, but Ethan swore there were a few twitches at the corners. He kept his arm curled around Cleo as he held out a hand to shake Ethan's. "Gil Grayson."

As all the rest of the men who adored Cleo, this one didn't appear as afraid of Ethan as he should have. Ethan squeezed.

Gil winced.

Cleo frowned. "Ethan, this is a very old friend of mine." She dragged her old friend over the threshold and into their living room, leaving Ethan to trail behind. "Come sit down, Gil," she said.

They shared the couch.

Ethan shared a menacing look with Gil.

Gil looked as if he wanted to laugh again.

Ethan cleared his throat. "So, you're an old friend of Cleo's?"

His wife was staring at him, her expression puzzled. What did she think? That he wouldn't care that her beautiful curves and her full lips had been so close to another man?

Gil shot a look at Cleo. "One of the oldest, I think."

"He knocked me down on my very first day in school," she explained, her amethyst eyes warming.

The other man flicked a long finger on Cleo's nose. "Because you had the cutest little braids. I had to get your attention somehow."

She laughed. "So that was it. The braids. Maybe I shouldn't have gotten rid of them."

Gil had a dimple, Ethan realized with disgust. It poked a hole in his cheek when he smiled ever-so-charmingly at Cleo. "You don't need braids to get my attention, sweetheart."

She nodded in agreement, still amused. "No, you're right. You noticed me for more practical reasons. Like math homework? Biology assignments? Tell Ethan that without me you wouldn't have made it through high school."

Gil looked up at Ethan, his face serious. "Without Cleo I wouldn't have made it through high school. I wouldn't have *gone* to school."

Cleo's brows snapped together. "Oh, stop."

Gil covered one of her hands with his. "It's true, Cleo. I was on a downhill slide. But you dragged me to the top of the hill with you every day."

Cleo appeared unconvinced. "That's nice of you to say, Gil, but—"

"It's true," he said implacably. "That's why when Mom told me things had been hairy for you lately, I thought I better check in. Maybe this time *you* need me."

Oh, no, buster. That was all that Ethan was going to take. No way was he just going to stand here while another man offered to be what his wife needed.

He stepped forward, that fire inside him heating up. "*I'll* be taking care of Cleo."

Gil's brows rose. "Yeah?"

Ethan stared pointedly at the man's hand, the hand that was still touching Cleo's. *"Yeah."*

"Stop being so silly," Cleo said.

To him.

Ethan stared back at her. "What?"

"Stop being so silly," she said again. "Why would you be rude to Gil?"

Ethan took a calming breath and explained to her slowly, rationally, "Because I'm your husband and I'll be damned if I'm going to let one of your lovesick swains waltz into *our* house and claim he's going to take care of you."

Cleo's forehead wrinkled. "What lovesick swains are you talking about?"

"Let's see." Ethan ticked them off on his fingers. "There was John and Jeremy and Stuart," he said, naming all the men he'd met in Whitehorn that couldn't wait to get their hands on Cleo. "And now there's Gil."

"None of those men is the least lovesick for me." She appealed to her brown-eyed "old friend." "Right, Gil?" But she didn't wait for him to agree with her. "Ethan, you know me. I'm the practical, sensible girl who's friends with all the guys. None of them ever really *wanted* me."

Ethan's eyes widened as he listened to his adorable, practical, sensible, capable but featherheaded wife. Only when it came to men, of course, but a featherhead all the same. "Cleo—"

Gil cleared his throat. "I think I might be able to help out here."

Ethan crossed his arms over his chest and narrowed his gaze at the other man. "I'm a little suspicious of your help," he said.

"Ethan!"

"He's right, Cleo," Gil said.

The featherhead scrunched her face up again. "About what?"

Both Ethan and Gil sighed.

Gil spoke first. "We all loved you, Cleo. Wanted you." He shrugged. "All those men Ethan mentioned, and some others besides."

She made another face. "I introduced at least half of those men Ethan named to their wives."

"Whom they only fell in love with after getting over you. After finally accepting the fact that you weren't going to give your heart to them."

She was staring at Gil, speechless.

"Really, Cleo. We used to joke about having our own club. 'Those Who Have Loved and Lost Cleo.'"

She shook her head. "No."

"And there are some of us, including me, who haven't ever gotten over—"

"Thank you, I believe she's heard enough." Ethan dragged Gil up from the couch by the elbow. As much as he was grateful to the guy for getting Cleo's attention at last, he wasn't feeling so kind as to let him try another round of "Take Me, I'm Yours."

Ethan steered Gil to the door. "I owe you," he muttered.

Gil dug his feet in once they reached the front door. "I mean what I was trying to say." His brown eyes went hard. "I'll be watching to see if you screw up."

Ethan looked at his wife, still sitting stunned and beautiful on the couch. "Don't hold your breath, friend. I love her more than you and anyone else in your little club. And she's never going to forget it."

The door closed behind Gil with a satisfying snap. Just to be on the safe side, Ethan turned the lock. Then he approached Cleo.

And found his feelings for her were rising in a big lump in his throat. He knelt on the floor in front of her. "Cleo," he said, his voice hoarse. "Do you understand now?"

She laughed a little shakily. "I don't know."

He stroked back her hair with his hand, aware he was trembling, just as she had been in the hospital. "No man has ever wanted you because you're practical or sensible or any of those things. They haven't wanted to just be your friend. They've only *settled* for being your friend."

A flush rose on her cheeks and he wanted to kiss them and her nose and her forehead and her lips and everywhere else he could reach.

"*You* wanted me because I'm practical and sensible. You said so," she pointed out.

Ethan groaned. "I'm an ass, Cleo." Maybe he didn't deserve her. "I was trying to come up with some plausible explanation for why I crossed five states to marry myself a convenient wife."

She lifted a hand toward him, but brought it back to her lap without touching him. "Is there an implausible explanation?"

He sucked in a breath. Maybe she wasn't such a

featherhead when it came to men. Because that was the biggest, most pointed question she could have asked.

The one he'd ducked and dodged for the three months they'd been apart and the two months they'd been married.

He stared straight into her amethyst eyes. "I fell in love with you, Cleo. Instantly, I think."

When he confessed that to her, he'd imagined a dozen reactions, but not the one she had. Cleo recoiled from him and looked as if he'd slapped her. "What?" she whispered.

He swallowed. "Last January. At the bed-and-breakfast. Do you remember how we met?"

"We bumped into each other," she said, as if the words were dragged from her.

"I looked down at you, at this curvy, warm, beautiful, amethyst-eyed witch and I thought someone had dropped something on my head. I was dizzy."

She didn't respond.

"And not one day went by after that I didn't hope to catch a glimpse of you, or talk to you. When I had to go back to Houston I had arguments with myself every day. I had to force my hand off the phone a dozen times."

She bit her lip. "Why didn't you want to love me?"

Oh, God. The hurt in her voice twisted Ethan's

heart. How could he have done this? How could he have caused pain to this woman?

And then he realized the most horrible truth of all. He could lose her. He could love her, and he could lose her.

He might find himself part of Gil's club, after all.

"Cleo," he said hastily, his brain spinning and whirling as it did at the conference table. What's the best way to present his case? What does the adversary want to hear? What words would best persuade her?

His mind went blank.

And from somewhere else, the truth arose. "It's easier not to love, Cleo. You can't get hurt—with a fist or with words. I thought that was the best way to live. And, hell, I was a success in anyone's eyes, including my own."

He raked his hand through his hair. "And then when I felt that...*thing* for you, I thought I was wrong to pursue you. You were a woman with heart, obviously, and I had managed to squeeze mine to nothing. I thought I didn't have the emotions to offer you."

"And then came Jonah."

He nodded. "And he desperately needed someone who had emotions, who had love. I instantly thought of you. I *wanted* you, all the while still telling myself that it was for Jonah's sake. All the while still thinking that what was beating inside me wouldn't be enough for you."

She reached out, and her fingertips touched his chest. He felt them through the thick material of his sweatshirt and he couldn't read their meaning, or what was written on her face. "What changed?" she whispered.

"I didn't think you or Jonah really needed me, Cleo," he said, his voice hoarse with honesty. "But in the hospital, I was able to comfort you, and comfort him. Not just provide for you both, you understand. You needed me. And I was there."

There was something in her eyes that was giving him hope, giving him strength. He caught her hand against his chest and flattened her palm over his heart. "It's bigger because of you, Cleo."

She threw herself at him.

He was unprepared, so they both crashed to the living room floor and his head hit the hardwood. The shooting pain didn't stop him from sinking his fingers into her hair and angling her face for his kiss.

She threw herself into that, too, but when they both came up for air, her eyes were worried. "Did I hurt you?"

He shook his head. "I was afraid you might, but then you came into my arms."

Her delectable lips pursed. "Your head, silly. Did you hurt your head?"

"I have no idea. I think you better take me to bed and check me out. Thoroughly."

Her lips twitched. But then her face sobered. "You love me?"

"I do. I will. I'll vow it all over again in front of a thousand people if you want me to. Particularly in front of that large fan club of yours. I want them to know some man has finally and forever leashed Cleo."

She wrinkled her nose. "'Leashed'?"

He smiled. "You're a menace to men, honey. It's the least I could do."

She pursed her lips again. He could tell the feather-head still didn't quite understand how many hearts she'd broken. But he was damn glad his wasn't one of them. A little doubt lingered in her eyes. "Are you sure you don't mind that I'm not so practical, so..."

"Capable?" he supplied.

She nodded, and he swiftly exchanged places with her so she was on the bottom and he was on top. He insinuated his hips into the warm notch of her thighs. "Mmm," he said, savoring the sensation. "I don't mind at all. I have big plans to keep you busy with some very impractical, very sexy activities."

She smiled dreamily up at him and linked her hands around his neck to pull him down for another kiss. "Is that so?"

He resisted, just long enough to get in the last word. "Oh, yeah. And I'm going to make sure you're incapable of speech for long nights of our long, happy marriage."

Ethan let himself be drawn down to her mouth. And then he took her to their bedroom where they made love.

When it was all over, he was the one made incapable of speech. But when she was able to whisper "I love you" and he only mouthed the words in return, he knew by her stunning smile that she understood.

* * * * *

Harlequin® *Romance*

MARGARET WAY

In the Australian Billionaire's Arms

Handsome billionaire David Wainwright isn't about to let his favorite uncle be taken for all he's worth by mysterious and undeniably attractive florist Sonya Erickson.

But David soon discovers that Sonya's no greedy gold digger. And as sparks sizzle between them, will the rugged Australian embrace the secrets of her past so they can have a chance at a future together?

*Don't miss this incredible new tale,
available in April 2011
wherever books are sold!*

Harlequin®

A *Romance* FOR EVERY MOOD™

www.eHarlequin.com

HRI7722

Harlequin Blaze
red-hot reads

Sunny, sensual Hawaiian spring break…again!

Three best girlfriends are recapturing an amazing spring-break vacation they had a decade ago.

First on the beach is former attorney and all-around good girl Mia Butterfield. Meeting up with her boyfriend of old is a bust, so she's shocked when her hero turns out to be someone she'd never have expected…

Find out who it is in
SECOND TIME LUCKY
by acclaimed author
Debbi Rawlins

Available from Harlequin Blaze® April 2011

Part of the sensual miniseries,
Spring Break

Part 2: Delicious Do-Over (May)

Harlequin®

A *Romance* FOR EVERY MOOD™

www.eHarlequin.com

HB79607

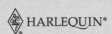

SPECIAL EDITION

Life, Love, Family and Top Authors!

In April, Harlequin Special Edition features
four *USA TODAY* bestselling authors!

FORTUNE'S JUST DESSERTS
by *MARIE FERRARELLA*

Follow the latest drama featuring the ever-powerful
and passionate Fortune family.

YOURS, MINE & OURS
by *JENNIFER GREEN*

Life can't get any more chaotic for Amanda Scott.
Divorced and a single mom, Amanda had given up on
the knight-in-shining-armor fairy tale until a friendship
with Mike becomes something a little more....

THE BRIDE PLAN (*SECOND-CHANCE BRIDAL* MINISERIES)
by *KASEY MICHAELS*

Finding love and second chances for others is
second nature for bridal-shop owner Chessie.
But will *she* finally get her second chance?

THE RANCHER'S DANCE
by *ALLISON LEIGH*

Return to the Double C Ranch this month—where love, loss
and new beginnings set the stage for Allison Leigh's latest title.

*Look for these titles and others in April 2011
from Harlequin Special Edition, wherever books are sold.*

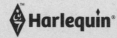

Harlequin®

A *Romance* FOR EVERY MOOD™

nocturne™

*Dark and sinfully delicious, Michelle Hauf's
Of Angels of Demons series continues to explore
the passionate world of angels and demons....*

FALLEN
BY MICHELLE HAUF

Fallen Angel Cooper has a steep price to pay, now that he walks the
earth among humans. Wherever the Fallen walk, a demon is not far
behind, intent upon slaying the Fallen in order to claim their own soul.
However, this particular demon strays from her mission, becoming
enamored with the mysterious Fallen Angel. Destined to remain bitter
enemies, the two find themselves entangled in a risky relationship—
with those who want to destroy them hot on their trail.

"Hauf delivers excitement, danger and romance in a way only she can!"
—#1 *New York Times* bestselling author Sherrilyn Kenyon

Available in April 2011, wherever books are sold.

Look for the next installment in the
Of Angels and Demons miniseries August 2011.

HNMH61856